Tina Wells

with Stephanie Smith

Random House 🏠 New York

Text and illustrations copyright © 2021 by Tina Wells
Cover art and interior illustrations by Brittney Bond

All rights reserved. Published in the United States by Random House
Children's Books, a division of Penguin Random House LLC, New York.

Random House and the colophon are registered trademarks of
Penguin Random House LLC.

Visit us on the Web! rhcbooks.com

Educators and librarians, for a variety of teaching tools, visit us at
RHTeachersLibrarians.com

Library of Congress Cataloging-in-Publication Data is available upon request.
ISBN 978-0-593-37829-8 (trade) — ISBN 978-0-593-37830-4 (lib. bdg.) —
ISBN 978-0-593-37831-1 (ebook)

Printed in the United States of America
10 9 8 7 6 5 4 3 2 1
First Edition

For Phoebe, my little bestie

CHAPTER ONE

I don't know everything about life yet, but I know at least one thing is true—life's easier when you make people happy.

You want to get good grades? Tell teachers what they want to hear. Want your friends to like you? Tell them you love their clothes and their hair and their moms' cooking. Want your parents to be happy? Do what they say. Follow their rules. Happy parents equals extra dessert and cool toys and fun vacations. And, most importantly, love.

Making people happy is what I'm good at. Sometimes that means not telling people the whole truth. Or telling them no truth at all. Not because I'm trying to be mischievous! In fact, I don't like to make trouble—but it always finds me somehow. Like the time I tried to compliment my best friend Nia on a pair of shoes she was wearing. I said they made her feet look "too long." She was mad at me for a week. I vowed to say only nice things about her feet no matter what.

Or the time I accidentally knocked over the mailbox when Dad asked me to take out the trash. Instead of walking it to the corner, I put the trash bag on my old wagon to roll it down the driveway. I had the wagon aimed perfectly at the mailbox to stop its roll, but it smacked into the pole harder than I expected, knocking the mailbox over at a forty-five-degree angle. Oops! I went inside and pretended nothing happened. But the next morning, Dad was furious. His eyebrows came together in the middle of his forehead. "Stupid garbage trucks! I'm going to find out who did this and get them fired," he said. I stood there, silent. What if he found out it was me? Would he fire me as his daughter? I kept my mouth shut. He fixed the mailbox and forgot about it in a few days, thankfully.

Or the time my mother asked me if I knew what the "birds and the bees" was, and I told her the truth—"No. Should I?" This led to one of the most uncomfortable conversations of my life about boys and girls and babies and . . . *ugh!* I get the heebie-jeebies every time I think about it!

I've found in my brief eleven years on this earth that the truth isn't always necessary. Tell people what they want to hear. Smile and nod. No one gets hurt. And that is how I planned to get through the sixth grade, through middle school, and through the rest of my life.

✦

It was the Sunday of Labor Day weekend, two days before the end of summer vacation. But in Featherstone Creek, a suburb of Atlanta, the weather stays warm through fall—so it still feels just a bit like summer outside. Mom, Dad, and I got back home from our house at Lake Lanier, about an hour's drive away, late at night— just in time for me to unload my bags, eat a spoonful of peanut butter, put on my pajamas, and immediately pass out. I don't even remember if I brushed my teeth. I slept like I hadn't slept for ten years, and I didn't wake up until I heard the chime notification from Nia's text on my phone.

NIA: You there? We're coming at 5 p.m. today.

I jumped out of bed and got dressed. My best friends Nia Shorter and Olive Banks were coming over for one last summer barbecue before school started. We were going to celebrate as if it were our birthdays and New Year's

Eve combined. After tonight, we had only one more day of no homework, no teachers, no alarms to wake up to before . . . *it begins.*

"It" being our first day of the sixth grade and our first day at Featherstone Creek Middle School.

We were no longer grade-schoolers. This was middle school. Prime time. The big leagues. At FCMS, we needed to bring our A games. We needed to make a great—scratch that, *legendary*—impression from day one and live up to the legacies that our parents and grandparents had created for us. Or else our parents would be disappointed. Our neighbors wouldn't like us. Teachers wouldn't like us. Then colleges wouldn't like us. And we wouldn't get degrees. And then we wouldn't be able to get good jobs, and we'd have no money or friends or husbands, and we'd be living on our parents' couches forever, surviving on chicken wings and Flamin' Hot Cheetos. And then we'd become embarrassments to our families. If, at that point, our families still claimed us.

Okay, maybe not all these things would happen if we didn't rock middle school. I tend to overthink things sometimes . . . just part of my charm, I guess? I don't really like Cheetos anyway!

I straightened up my bedroom, which was next to Dad's office. I kept my room nice and neat so my parents wouldn't be tempted to come in and rifle through my things, like my journals or my laptop or—*gasp*—my phone.

If they thought I kept my room in order, they'd think I kept my life in order, too. I smoothed my sheets and comforter and arranged all the pillows from large to small against the headboard. I cleaned my desk and straightened my framed photos of me and Nia and me and my BFF Chloe Lawrence-Johnson, who I've known since I was a baby but who moved to Los Angeles with her family last year. I went into my bathroom and put away the bottles of leave-in conditioner and edge gel I used on my hair today to put it up into a high braided bun—my go-to hairstyle for a summertime barbecue. Tomorrow, the day before school, is wash day.

By the time I made it downstairs, my stomach was already rumbling, and my mom and dad were almost set getting food ready for the barbecue. My dad, wearing an old Howard University T-shirt and jeans, stood at the kitchen counter over a huge platter of chicken covered with barbecue sauce. My dad is a lawyer. He went to school with Nia's dad at THE Howard University, aka the Harvard of the HBCUs, aka the Mecca, according to Dad. He practically screams "H-U! You *knowwwwww*!" if anyone merely thinks about Howard in the same room as him. And he has big plans for his little girl to follow in his footsteps. Every. Single. One. He runs a law firm together with Nia's dad in downtown Featherstone Creek, with their last names on the front of their office building.

Dad wants me to either run his firm when he retires or head into politics, like Madam Vice President Kamala Harris ("H-U '86!" my dad screams at any mention of her name). I like wearing and buying nice clothes, and I definitely love MVP Harris, but I don't know how I feel about arguing with people all the time, which is what legal stuff seems to be about, at least to me. And those suits they wear in court. They're so stiff and itchy! And lady lawyers have to wear pantyhose even on hot summer days in Atlanta. Meanwhile, I get uncomfortable in jean shorts in July sometimes!

My mom is a doctor who delivers babies for all the moms in town. She works a lot, but she gets to hold babies all the time, which sounds awesome. Her family grew up in Featherstone Creek, and most of them started businesses here. Her dad, my granddad, has a family practice on Main Street. He's our family doctor and Nia's family doctor. And the doctor for half of my sixth-grade class.

My parents always mean well—they want the best for me—and I want to make them happy. Because when they're happy, the house is happy. We eat ice cream and go to the Crab Shack for dinner. And spend more time at our lake house, and my mom and I get our nails done together at the salon. And my dad laughs with his mouth wide open, and when he laughs, everyone else laughs. When my parents aren't happy, there are rain clouds, and boiled brussels sprouts for dinner, and my mom calls me by my full name—"June Naomi Jackson!"—in a high-pitched voice, and my dad's eyebrows come together on his forehead like one long, hairy caterpillar. The eyebrows scare. The. Life. Out. Of. Me.

So, if me playing field hockey, going to Howard, and being a lawyer are what's going to make them happy, then that's what I'll do. Or at least I'll *say* it's what I want to do. But a girl has a right to her own opinions. And a right to change her own opinions, too. Even if she keeps them to herself, which I am very used to doing.

At 5:00 p.m. the doorbell rang. Mr. and Mrs. Shorter and Nia stood at the door. Mrs. Shorter held a large Tupperware bowl of potato salad for dinner. "Hello, June, how are you, baby? Oh, you're getting so tall," she said.

"Hi, Mrs. Shorter. My mom is in the kitchen."

"Smells good back there," Mr. Shorter said, giving me a gentle hug. Nia's parents walked toward the back of the house. Nia put an arm around me. "Girl! I thought you'd never come back!"

"We texted every day I was gone!" I said. She and Olive and I texted multiple times a day, all through summer. We basically knew where each other was at every second of the day. Nia rolled her eyes and smiled. We both giggled and ran upstairs to my bedroom. I flopped onto the bed, and Nia followed me, placing her bag down next to her.

"Sixth grade," I said. "Finally, a place where I can really express myself." I could use different-colored gel pens for my homework. Explore creative writing, join the school paper, really voice my opinions on big issues, like going vegan and saving the animals. Maybe I'd run for student body president. And I could even buy my own lunch! Freedom—I'd *literally* be able to taste it. "I'll be glad to get out from under my parents' wing," I said.

"You act as if you're going off to college," Nia said.

"They still feed you and give you an allowance." Ugh. She was *technically* right. But at least I could choose one of my own daily meals at school! That would be a taste of freedom—it had to count for something.

"Did you read the books on the summer reading list?" I asked.

"I only made it through one," Nia answered.

"Which one?"

"The shortest one. Something about the guy with the dog. It said the reading was optional."

"Optional, but encouraged," I said resolutely. I chose to read half the books on the list, though they, too, were the shortest ones. Even if teachers weren't assigning the book list as a requirement, it could only make them happy to know you did some of the reading. It might help me get in good with these teachers from the beginning. I could use all the early bonus points I could get.

A knock on the door interrupted our conversation. "It's me," Olive called out. "Sorry we're late. Mom couldn't decide what to wear. What's going on?" she asked as she opened the door, walked in, and plopped onto my bed.

"We're talking about school," I said.

"Yeah? I'm excited. Orchestra starts up again next week. I learned how to play Michael Jackson's 'Beat It' on the viola this summer."

"On to the most important topic," Nia interrupted. "What are you going to wear for the first day?"

I stood up and threw open the doors to my closet. Mom and I had gone shopping for new clothes the week before we went to Lake Lanier. She took me to the same stores where she's bought clothes for me since I was four.

"This would look so cute on you," Mom had said, holding up a pleated skirt with a printed pattern of teddy bears with their paws in honey jars. It looked like what preschoolers in the Alps might wear as part of their school wardrobe. I hated it.

I clenched my teeth. "It's cute, Mom, very cute." She tossed it into the shopping cart. I groaned internally, but I figured if I let her pick out one thing she liked, maybe I could get what I really wanted.

I wanted to go to stores that aligned more with my sense of style. This place called Fit sold women's clothes and accessories and just about every item I'd seen on some influencer or celebrity on Instagram. I pointed to a dress on a mannequin in the store window as we passed by. "I saw this dress on that dark-haired Disney Channel actress you like, and she's my age."

"Yeah, but she's an actress, playing a role. You are in sixth grade, and I don't know if I want you wearing that. It's a bit . . . mature."

"That's the point," I said. "*I'm* a bit mature now." I'm in sixth freaking grade! I am almost in a training bra! Can't she see I'm practically a *woman*?

I walked inside. There was a white sleeveless blouse

with a large bow at the neck that could pair with everything in my closet and still make me look sophisticated, even with that horrible teddy bear skirt my mom bought. But I really wanted to wear it with the pair of distressed jeans on display that had a few holes around the knees that . . . oh, look at that . . . came in my size.

She ended up buying me the blouse on the condition that I wear a sweater or jacket over it. She got her baby skirt, and I got my blouse. Everybody was happy. *Compromise.*

"So, the first day of school," Nia said. She and Olive looked at my clothes hanging neatly in my closet. "Are we doing the skinny jeans with the oversized T-shirt thing? Maybe with those Air Force 1s? Or with a shiny ballet flat? You need something that will really make a statement on the first day."

"I want something that says I'm . . . interesting," I said thoughtfully.

"Soooo, black on black on black?" Nia smirked.

"Or maybe a caftan?" Olive said.

"A caftan?" Nia asked.

"Yeah, like what my grandmother wears exclusively from April through October. She says they let her skin breathe," Olive said. "Whatever that means."

"Fashion inspiration from your grandmother may not be a good first look for the sixth grade," I said. We would have two-point-five seconds to make an impression on our fellow students and teachers at Featherstone Creek Middle School that would define how people saw us for the rest of our lives. At least that is what my dad told me about first impressions.

"Nia, what are you wearing?" Olive asked.

"Probably a skirt and my new denim jacket. Took me forever to get those rhinestones glued on, so you better believe I'm going to show off my work."

Man, why couldn't I design my own clothes, like Nia? What if I had the potential to be the next great American fashion designer like Vera Wang or Zac Posen and I'd never know it because my mom still picks out my clothes? All that potential, undiscovered. We were doing the world a disservice by not letting me pick out my own clothes!

"Girls! Food is almost ready!" my mom called from downstairs.

Nia and Olive moved toward the closet and quickly ruffled through my clothes. Nia found a white Vans T-shirt. "Pair this with that black denim skirt and you're set."

"Done," I said. "Statement made. Says 'sixth grade, here I am.'"

We gave each other high fives, then went downstairs and walked toward the back of the house for dinner.

✦

The sun was getting low in the sky, and the fireflies were just starting to make their appearance as we all gathered around the large picnic table on our patio for dinner. Olive, Nia, and I sat on the far side of the long dining table. Dad placed platters of grilled chicken and steaks in the middle of the table, along with big bowls of potato salad and fruit salad.

"Dig in, fam," Dad said. Several hands reached eagerly for the food. My mom kicked off the conversation. "Girls, are you excited for sixth grade?"

"Yes," we said in unison.

"I know that June is looking forward to field hockey," Dad said. That wasn't exactly true. *He* was excited for me to play field hockey. I had never even played before. But I went along with team tryouts because it made him happy. If I told him I didn't want to, he might think I was defying

him. And then, I'd get the eyebrows. Must. Avoid. The. Eyebrows. "Do any of you girls play sports?"

"I'm going to play basketball again this year," Nia said.

"And I'm still in dance," said Olive. "And I play viola in the orchestra."

"Wonderful," my mom responded. "June, I wished you would have taken up ballet when you were younger. It always looks good to the private schools when you have some sort of performing arts background."

"Yeah, Mom, but hard to squeeze in ballet between those field hockey practices," I said, half joking, trying to butter up my dad.

"Sixth grade," Mrs. Shorter said. "I can't believe that these babies are in sixth grade already. Where does the time go?"

"Howard's just around the corner," my dad joked. I smiled, laughing along as if I were cosigning his college prep plans. Howard's not a bad choice. But it's also not the *only* choice.

Dinner continued, with the conversation finally breaking up between the sixth graders and the adults. As the bottoms of everyone's plates became visible again, my mom announced, "Who wants cake?"

At our house, every Sunday dinner in the summertime ended with Mom's 7UP cake. It's a Southern tradition. A Jackson family tradition. A tradition I could easily skip.

The cake was a bit dense for my taste. But I didn't dare tell my mom that. Telling your mom her dessert is bad is basically telling her you don't love her. Or to never make you a cake again. I like cake. And I love my mom. So I lie.

My mother cut thick slices for my friends. They grabbed their forks and dug in. "June?"

"Yes, Mom, thank you! You know how much I love your cake!" I said. Mom placed a slice in front of me. I stabbed at the heavy slice until it turned into a mound of crumbs. I took a few bites just for show and tried not to grimace. The sugary icing wasn't too bad, though.

"How's the cake, girls?"

"Great, Mom," I said. She smiled. I smiled. *Smile and nod, June. Smile and nod.*

The adults lingered around the picnic table until the sun dipped below the tree line and darkness set in. The lightning bugs danced around our backyard with abandon, and Nia, Olive, and I skipped through the grass, laughing and singing along to our favorite songs until the parents said it was time for Nia and Olive to go.

"I don't want to say goodbye," I started to whine loudly. I felt the emotions bubble up.

"It's not goodbye, it's see you later," Olive said.

"It's 'see you in two days,' June," Nia said. "Get a grip."

We gave each other a group hug. "See you then," I said. Dinner was over. My time to run free, laugh, dance around, and be silly would soon be over, too. In two days I'd have to grow up, put on my game face, and become a poised young woman entering a more mature phase of her life. It was time to get serious. Sixth grade was almost here.

CHAPTER TWO

L ee Noel had been coming over to our house in Featherstone Creek since he was in first grade. We're friends. *Just* friends. Though, if he decided we should be girlfriend and boyfriend and plan to go to the same colleges and then get married and live happily ever after, I would not object. But he had no idea how I felt. And I planned to keep it that way until he confessed his feelings for me. I couldn't handle the rejection if he didn't care about me that way. And I didn't want to make things weird. Why mess up a good friendship between us with all those . . . feelings?

Lee and I had gone to different preschools, but we met when we both started going to kindergarten together. He moved in with his grandparents then, because his parents traveled so much—both his mom and dad were in the military. Our families figured out we both had summer houses on Lake Lanier, and since then we've tried to co-ordinate our weekends at the lake houses together. Lee and I always met up on early Saturday mornings to ride our bikes to the main boat ramp of the lake. We'd talk to fishermen and old locals and the woman who ran the local bakery, who sometimes gave us free cinnamon rolls if we were lucky. We would walk along the lake picking flowers, debating music, pondering the seven wonders of the world ("But how does your dad know how to do the Renegade?" Lee asked one day. "You certainly didn't teach him." "Anyone can learn anything on the internet," I replied.)

Even though we'd just seen each other a few days ago, Lee came over tonight before the first day of school—mostly because he hadn't been at Sunday dinner and had missed out on my mom's 7UP pound cake. He always had a slice whenever Mom made the cake. Sometimes he took two.

"Hi, Dr. Jackson," Lee said as my mother opened the door.

"Hello, Lee. How you doing?"

"Fine. Heard you had a barbecue with the girls last night."

"Yes, we had Nia's family and Olive's family over. You know them, right?"

"Yeah, I do," Lee said. Then he slowly rubbed his chin.

"So, if there was a barbecue, then there's gotta be some cake, right?"

"In the kitchen, Lee," my mom said, cocking her head. "June's in there, too."

Lee walked behind my mother toward the kitchen. He had on a tattered Atlanta Falcons T-shirt and oversized jeans. He'd just gotten a haircut—those were some sharp lines in that hair. "What's going on, June?" he said.

"Hey," I said. "That your school fade you rockin'?"

"You know it," he said. "Gotta be fresh to death for the first day. I heard there's cake."

"You say that every time you come over."

"There's always cake when I come over."

I pointed toward the kitchen island, where half of the cake was sitting on a cake stand.

"I'll cut you a slice, dear," Mom said. "June, you want a slice?"

If I didn't take some cake, she'd be disappointed. *Take the cake, June. Keep her happy. Eating the cake equals telling her "I love you."*

"Sure, Mom," I replied.

Lee sat down at the kitchen table with his piece of cake. "So, ready for school tomorrow?" I asked him.

"Yeah, I got all my school supplies already. I kind of don't want to go back, though."

"Why not?"

"Because I'd rather go fishing or be outside. Way more fun out there."

"Yeah, right? I'd much rather be, like, fishing or something," I blurted out. I don't know why. I love the lake. I love boats. I don't love worms and hooks and dead fish. But Lee does, so I could pretend to like fishing, too.

I quickly turned the subject back to school. "I'm a little nervous myself," I said. "School will be harder, and Dad wants me to try out for field hockey—*and* I thought about joining the school paper this year. Field hockey will be in season until November, but the paper is a yearlong commitment. Plus, schoolwork."

"Yeah, but you got that. You always handle everything."

Inside I preened. It's a lot of hard work to look like you're handling everything. But it's good to know at least Lee thinks I've got everything under control.

"Let's go outside. I don't want to miss when the lightning bugs come out." Lee put his plate on the kitchen counter, next to where my mom was quickly washing a few dishes. "Thank you, Dr. Jackson."

We walked toward the backyard and climbed onto the trampoline. I can jump high and do a front flip, but I cannot for the life of me stick my landings for my backflips. My dad is always telling me not to flip, because I might hurt myself. I can imagine my dad now: "Then there goes field hockey!"

It was so easy to get caught up in my parents' future plans for me, so I thought back to simpler times. When we were younger, Lee and I tried to catch as many lightning bugs as we could in mason jars or lab jars Mom brought back from the hospital. One time I begged my mom to let us look at bugs underneath the microscope in the lab of the hospital. Everything was so much easier back then. No drama, no worries about school or my career or making my parents happy. I wish we could re-create it. . . .

"Should we try to catch some lightning bugs?" I asked Lee.

"I'm too full to run," Lee said, plopping down on the trampoline, his legs sprawled out in front of him. "Let's just watch them fly."

We lay back on the trampoline, the black bottom mat warm from the sun. Lying there with Lee felt easy-breezy. We watched lightning bugs dance around us. The sky went from blue to gray to pink to dark. We listened to crickets and faint car horns in the distance. I closed my eyes for a moment, imagining myself floating up to the sky and flying through the stars, looking down at my house, my parents, the world. What if I could come up here and escape everything from time to time? Escape chores. Escape rules. Escape worrying about perfect grades. Or about saying the right thing. What if I could come here and release all my innermost thoughts without anyone hearing me? Or if I could listen to other people's innermost thoughts? This could be my own little safe haven. My happy haven. I closed my eyes a bit tighter.

I kept my eyes closed for as long as possible. Tonight, in this moment, I didn't have a care in the world. But tomorrow the lighting bugs would be gone, summer would be over, and Featherstone Creek Middle School would be open for business. A new day would begin.

After Lee left, I gathered my school supplies for the next day—fresh colored gel pens, Post-it notes, notebooks, and highlighters—and tucked them into my brand-new book bag. I was making room in my bathroom cabinet for the new moisturizer and face wash I'd bought. My phone buzzed just as I broke open the packaging. Nia.

I swiped to answer the FaceTime.

"Hey, girl! You ready?"

"Yeah, I guess. Lee just left," I said.

"Leeeeee," Nia said. "Last night before our first big day and you spent it with Leeee."

"Calm down, we're just friends! Just like you and me," I said.

"C'mon, you've never thought about him as more than a friend?"

I got all warm inside and sweaty. "No!" I said, maybe too forcefully.

Nia raised one eyebrow. "Sure. Anyway," she said, "do you have that gold charm bracelet you borrowed from me a few weeks ago? Before you went to the lake? I want to wear it tomorrow with my outfit."

I froze. Oh man. I'd loved that bracelet ever since Nia got it for her birthday. And my best friend graciously let me borrow it for my time at the lake just because I asked, and because she knew I was responsible enough to return it. But I'd accidentally lost it when I jumped into the lake with Lee. He grabbed my wrist as he jumped, and his grip was a bit tighter than I'd expected. By the time I realized it, the bracelet had snapped off and was likely sitting at the bottom of the lake. My plan was to buy a replacement bracelet before Nia knew it was missing, but I hadn't had the time to shop yet, especially since we'd gotten back home so late.

"Um, yeah," I stammered, trying to think of a quick

white lie to tell her. "I haven't unpacked from the lake yet, but let me look around for it and bring it to you tomorrow." It was just to buy some time, and what she didn't know wouldn't hurt her.

"Aiight, I'll see you tomorrow. Eeek! So excited!" Nia said, seemingly forgetting about the bracelet for the moment.

"Yup! G'night!" I said, also excited. Also nervous. Also thinking about how I was going to replace Nia's bracelet. And thinking about Lee in some kind of way that made me smile and daydream while I brushed my teeth. I snapped back to reality once I felt bubbly toothpaste dripping down my chin. Then I washed my face, tucked myself into bed, and tried to get some rest before my first day at FCMS.

CHAPTER THREE

✦✦
✦

The first day of school came even faster than I'd expected. My alarm blared at 6:15 a.m. I grabbed my phone, read a message from Chloe that she'd sent late last night (**Good luck at school tomorrow! Let me know how it goes!**), and quickly swiped through Instagram, looking for something to make me smile. I found a meme of a cat impersonating a mom nagging her kids to get ready for school. How fitting.

I went to the bathroom to brush my teeth and wash my face, then unwrapped the scarf from around my head and pulled my hair back into a high ponytail. There were two headbands on my bathroom counter, a silk one and a rhinestone one. I looked in the mirror and slid the rhinestone one on.

"June, honey, come down and have a good breakfast before school," my mom called out. She walked up the stairs and stopped in front of the bathroom door. "You ready?"

"I just need to grab my clothes."

"I laid out your outfit on your bed already."

I cringed inside. I was really looking forward to wearing the outfit Nia had picked out for me. Mom walked toward my bedroom, expecting me to follow. I stood in front of my bed and the outfit she'd picked: the skirt with the teddy bears was on it, and a T-shirt with another teddy bear eating a plate of pasta. "C'mon, get dressed, and then we can have breakfast."

I bit my tongue. The outfit was great for dinner out with Winnie-the-Pooh, not for the first day of sixth grade! I turned toward the closet to look for the outfit Nia and Olive and I had discussed. But as soon as I took a step toward the closet, Mom stood in front of me. "Oh, you'll look so cute in this! It'll go great with your new backpack and new shoes."

I knew if I told Mom that I didn't like the clothes and that those shoes looked like something out of a JCPenney catalog from 2001, her heart would shatter. And she'd think I was ungrateful. And then she would go to her bedroom and cry all day, talking about how her little girl didn't love her anymore. And she would be so upset, she couldn't go to work, and then she wouldn't be able to deliver any other little girls for other moms, and her whole career would be over. Which, to my mom, basically would mean her whole *life* was over. I couldn't do that to her!

Well, I mean, she probably wouldn't cry—Mom was a pretty logical person who didn't really react that extremely to many things. She was a doctor, after all. Still, I didn't want to hurt her feelings over an outfit, even if it did make me miserable.

I grabbed the skirt and T-shirt and started putting the clothes on, gritting my teeth the whole time.

"Don't forget the socks, too. With the ruffles," she added.

Ruffled socks. I didn't know where in the world she had even found ruffled socks. I looked like I was eight years old. I felt like I was eight *months* old!

"I'll start the eggs," she said. She kissed me on the forehead and walked out of my bedroom, leaving me alone. I closed my eyes tight, afraid to think about the impression I was about to leave on Featherstone Creek Middle School for my first day of sixth grade—that I, June Jackson, was still too young and immature to pick out my own clothes, much less be considered a woman of substance on campus.

I trotted down the stairs toward the kitchen, the new shoes stiff and pinching my feet. Luisa, our housekeeper, had arrived and was starting on her daily routine. Mom scooped out scrambled eggs from a pan and spooned them onto a plate.

"Tasty stuff," Dad said, having already eaten. He tucked the last of his things into his briefcase. "Eat up before your first day, June. You need the fuel." He gave me a kiss on the cheek. "I'm off, see you tonight."

I ate breakfast quickly, interrupted only by my cell phone vibrating in my bag. Nia had sent me a text. **Hey girl, ready in ten minutes? Meet outside your driveway? Don't forget my bracelet!** I cringed. I was going to tell her I'd simply forgotten it at the lake house. Somewhat true. True enough to buy me some time to buy another bracelet.

Featherstone Creek Middle School was a short walk from my house. Now that we were in middle school, our parents said we could walk by ourselves without supervision as long as we stayed together. Olive lived a bit farther away, but she could walk to Nia's house and pick her up, then walk over to my house so we could head toward school together.

I grabbed my backpack and kissed my mom on the cheek. "You need anything, you call," Mom said. "I can't believe we're not taking you on your first day of school. These kids, growing so fast."

I bit my tongue. How could she think I was growing up when she was dressing me like a toddler? Is that what this was all about? She was trying to pretend I was still her baby?

"Nia, Olive, and I just want to be together on the first day."

"I get it," my mom said. "I can see you most of the way there from the back door anyway. I love you, baby."

I met Nia and Olive at the end of the driveway. Nia had on the denim jacket she had customized with rhinestones and sequins, a black T-shirt, black jeans, and new Nike sneakers. Olive was wearing a tie-dyed shirt and a maxi skirt. Both of them looked excited about the first day of school. "Heeeeey!" they said. Their eyes scanned my outfit. Their smiles faded.

"Ugh, Nia, I know, I forgot your bracelet," I lied.

"June, we have bigger problems," she said to me. "What happened to the other outfit we picked out for you?" Nia sounded incredulous.

"My mother is what happened to it," I said. "She had a vision of what she wanted me to wear, and this was it."

"It's not so bad," Olive said with a wince.

"Yes, it is," Nia said.

"Don't bother being polite," I said sarcastically to Nia.

"Sorry," Nia said. She looked me over head to toe. "Can you sneak in and grab the outfit we picked out, and come back out? And grab some proper socks. We can fix this."

I did as I was told. I walked back toward my house and through the garage, headed for the stairway in the back of the house. I made it to the base of the stairs undetected, when Mom suddenly spotted me out of the corner of her eye. "You're back? What happened?"

I froze, panicked. I came up with a quick excuse. "I forgot one of my notebooks."

I slunk up the stairs before the feeling of lying to her outright and running off could get worse. I bounded up the stairs two by two and quickly found the pair of purple-and-yellow Air Force 1s in the closet. I stuffed them in my backpack, then grabbed the Vans T-shirt, the denim skirt, and a pair of plain ankle socks from my drawer and went back downstairs. Nia and Olive were still on the driveway waiting for me.

"Got the goods?" Nia said.

"Yeah," I said.

"Okay, when we get around the corner, you'll change."

We walked quickly toward the end of the block and hung a right. There was a big hedge that blocked the view of traffic, large enough for us to huddle behind and re-style me. "Okay, first, take those ruffled socks off," Nia said. "Where did you get them, babyGap?"

I pulled the socks off and swapped out my black Mary Janes for the sneakers. Then Nia and Olive huddled around me. I pulled the black denim skirt on under my current skirt and undid the button on the teddy bear skirt to slide it down. I carefully pulled the teddy bear T-shirt over my head so I didn't mess up my hair, and then I quickly slid on the Vans T-shirt. I stuffed the old outfit into my backpack, made some adjustments, and threw my arms wide to present myself to Nia and Olive.

"Yasss! This looks way more schoolgirl chic!" Nia said. She took out her phone and took a full-length photo of me. I looked at myself in the photo. I felt so much happier in these clothes. The smile grew across my face, and my shoulders relaxed.

"Wow." I smiled as she showed me the picture. "Yes. Much better."

"Now you're ready for school," Olive said. *"Let's go!"*

◆

Featherstone Creek Middle School was a modern brick-and-glass building packed with about two hundred students in sixth, seventh, and eighth grades. The school sat back from the main street and had a long circular drive where buses and cars could drop students off.

We walked through the main entrance into a loud, crowded hallway. Kids milled about before the bell rang, and the mood was electric, especially among the sixth graders. The older kids didn't look as happy to be back in school. What did they have to be unhappy about? They were basically adults, and closer to freedom than I was!

We had been assigned our lockers and combinations earlier in summer, during middle school orientation. My locker was in the middle of the main hall. I stopped in front of it and took my backpack off. Olive's and Nia's lockers were farther down the main hallway, toward the middle of school. "We'll meet you at homeroom," Olive said, and they turned away.

I struggled to open my lock. I worked through the combination a few times, but the latch seemed to be stuck. I jiggered it harder and harder, until an older student noticed me. "Need a hand?" he said, smirking.

"Nah, I'm good," I told him, half-embarrassed, half lying. I blushed. This is not the calm and cool image I wanted to project on day one. I tried yanking on the latch again, but it still wouldn't budge.

"No sweat—watch," he said, and gently massaged the latch upward until it unlocked and the door swung open. "There ya go. Now, get some lip gloss or ChapStick or curl cream or anything slick you've got in your backpack to put on the latch. That'll keep it from sticking."

"Thanks," I said sheepishly. *Wow, June, could you be any greener?* I thought. He must have thought I was clueless. Even if he did, he was still polite enough to give me a nod as he continued walking down the hall. My face remained hot while I unpacked my books.

I watched Nia walk through the hallway like the lead singer of a girl group, confident and ready for whatever sixth grade had in store. "Hey, girl! How you doing?" she said to Kenya Barrett, a girl who lived on Nia's block. I was jealous of how effortless it seemed for her. I wish I could be that confident, that easily.

I dug out my tablet and the textbook for my math class from my backpack, and then shoved the backpack into the locker a little harder than necessary. The school had mailed the tablets home at the beginning of August for us to use in class and for our homework. I suppose we were lucky that we got them for free, but they added an extra pound or two to my backpack.

I walked through the crowd of kids hustling to class, hugging and talking excitedly after not seeing each other for several weeks. I recognized a few kids from Mill Creek Elementary, where I'd gone to grade school, like Lee's friend Alvin Abramson and Rachelle Knight, who somehow looked much taller than I last remembered.

Homeroom was just at the end of the hall, close to Olive's locker, so I stopped for a moment so we could head in together. It was surprisingly empty inside her locker, with plenty of room for her new books and pens. "Where's your viola and dance stuff?"

"My viola's in the band room," Olive said. "And dance starts next week." Which reminded me—how much equipment and athletic clothes was I going to have to lug back and forth because of field hockey? My stomach sank at the thought.

Olive and I walked into homeroom and grabbed desks next to each other. Just as we sat down, Nia strode in, walking fast toward the seat in front of me. "Girl, did you hear about the new girl in school?"

"Isn't everybody new?" I asked.

"No, girl, I mean *new*. Like she's from Boston or something. She's *new* new."

"Oh. No, haven't seen her."

"I think she might be that girl from—"

Just then, Mrs. Worth entered the room. She had brown shoulder-length hair that bounced as she talked. She took our attendance and made a half hour's worth of important announcements for the first day of class, like what to do if you're late, if you're sick, if you have to go to the bathroom. I took notes on all of this on the tablet while Nia looked bored (not one note taken) and Olive looked confused (not sure if she took enough notes).

From homeroom, we went to math. I was eager to get a good seat near the front so I could make frequent eye contact with the teacher, Mrs. Charles. If she saw that I was super interested in the lesson, maybe she'd be more interested in giving me a good grade.

After math, I had earth sciences, which was about, well, earth and geology and the weather, and included regular field trips outdoors to observe nature. I was stoked. Any excuse to get out of the classroom into the woods was a good one.

Then came social studies, or a study of what old people did back in the day to create the world we know. Mr. Brown said that one of those "optional but encouraged" books on the summer reading list would be discussed in the next few days of the class. But it was not one of the books I'd chosen to read at the lake before school started. Olive nodded when the teacher announced the news. She saw my worried face. "You didn't read the books?"

"I didn't read *this* one. The list said 'optional but encouraged.' I chose the shortest ones."

"I read them all," Olive said. "Don't worry, I'll give you my notes."

English comprehension was after social studies, and then there was lunch. Nia, Olive, and I walked together to the cafeteria, picked out a table that we hoped to make our regular seats, and bought the daily special, chili con carne, for lunch.

On my way out of the cafeteria, a flyer caught my eye and made me smile—a sign advertising the school newspaper (COME AND WRITE FOR THE FEATHERSTONE POST. WE MEET AND PITCH STORIES ON MONDAYS IN THE OFFICE. STORIES DUE WEDNESDAYS AND THURSDAYS). I already knew I wanted to join. The paper would give me an opportunity to make a name for myself. Share ideas! Maybe I'd get my own column! And those meetings fit in perfectly between my field hockey practices. I put my name on the sign-up list and planned on going to the first school newspaper meetup next week. I wondered what stories I could write first. An interview with the athletic director? Or maybe the eighth-grade football star?

All of a sudden, I felt an overwhelming urge to use the restroom. "I'll meet you all in class," I yelled, already heading in the opposite direction.

I beelined to the nearest bathroom, dashed into a stall, and made it onto the toilet just in time. I turned to grab the roll of toilet paper. Dang it! Empty! I had a few tissues in my bag, so I reached for it to fish them out. I removed my change purse, some nuts left over from lunch, and my T-shirt for field hockey to get to the Kleenex. I took out a few sheets and used them before standing and redressing. I reached for the handle to flush, but I accidentally knocked the empty paper cylinder into the toilet. The water was already swirling around the bowl, so I let it go, thinking the roll would disintegrate and schloop down the bowl.

But the toilet just stopped. The water started to rise higher in the bowl. I had to get to class. I panicked. I shoved my belongings back into my book bag, but as my slippery fingers grabbed my snacks, I accidentally knocked those into the bowl, too! Ack! Well, I certainly wouldn't be eating those almonds now!

I tried to flush it all away one more time. I crossed my fingers and hoped that one last flush would get it all to go down.

It seemed to work at first, the water spiraling toward the bottom of the bowl and disappearing. Suddenly, *whoososhshsh!* An explosion of water shot out of the toilet bowl and all over the floor. My shoes became wet, and I was positively soaked with embarrassment. So I did what any sensible, mature eleven-year-old would do. I decided to run and hide from my crime.

I peeked my head out of the stall and saw no one. I grabbed my backpack and ran water over my hands for three seconds, then yanked a paper towel off the roll and went for the exit, trying to dash out before anyone could see me there. But I wasn't fast enough.

A custodian stood at the front door, his eyes wide, surveying the mess that had been created by the toilet. "Good

God, what happened in here?" he asked. He looked at me. I should have confessed. I wanted to. But my face grew hot. I couldn't afford to get in trouble on the first day of middle school! My parents would put me on punishment for life! I just wanted to run. My lack of common sense and knowledge of how toilets work led me to say only one thing as I sprinted out of the bathroom: "I don't know!"

✦

After lunch we had mostly creative and arts classes, and at 2:45 p.m., school was over. For me, it was time to go to field hockey position tryouts. Dad was so into me joining the field hockey team that he had already sent video clips of me running around the park to Coach Dwight, who'd told my dad I had "natural ability." Which I'm guessing just means "long legs, good for running around." For me, field hockey didn't seem natural at all. Running up and down a field with sticks and swatting at a ball seemed dangerous. And there was no headgear! What if I got smacked in the face? Howard wouldn't accept me if I was missing all my teeth!

Field hockey practices would be three times a week starting the next week, and by Thursday afternoon they'd assign us potential positions on the team. There were games scheduled every Tuesday once the season started, and the season would go all the way through fall.

For practice, we were given a warm-up tee to work out in, but I had also brought my own workout clothes to change into before I hit the field. Our coach greeted the team and gave us a quick pep talk, then put us through a series of drills. For all my skepticism about my dad's encouragement for me to play, I couldn't believe how naturally the sport came to me. The footwork made me feel like I was dancing, moving to an effortless rhythm. And running down the field while moving the ball with a stick didn't seem nearly as tricky as I'd thought it would be. I'd practiced a little at home by swatting around an orange with a broom in my basement for kicks. But it was much smoother and way more satisfying to move around an opponent while racing toward a goal. I didn't quite want to admit it, but I could get into this.

We were done by 4:00 p.m. I headed to the locker room to change my clothes, back into the outfit that Nia had picked out for me. Mom was probably working late today, as usual, so she wouldn't be home when I got there, and I didn't want anyone to see me in that toddler uniform she'd chosen. I'd planned to walk home with Nia and Olive anyway. I dug my cell phone out of my bag, which I only turned on after school, since phones weren't allowed during class. My mom had sent a text. She was waiting outside for me. I **left work early just so I could pick you up from your first day.**

Oh no. What, were no babies born today in Featherstone Creek?

WAIT.

Mom was going to see that I wasn't wearing the outfit she'd picked out that morning.

I panicked. Instead of changing again, I threw my field hockey T-shirt over the clothes. The shirt came down almost to my knees, long enough to cover up that I wasn't wearing the skirt. Then I grabbed my bag and headed out. I texted Nia and Olive as I walked to the exit. **Don't wait up for me. Mom surprised me and is here to get me.**

When I got into the car, Mom was so excited to hear about my first day that she barely noticed that I wasn't wearing her approved outfit under the T-shirt.

"How were field hockey tryouts?" she asked.

"Good," I responded, and I meant it. At least I didn't need to lie about that. We were home in three minutes.

Day one done. Off to a strong start. Well, except that whole toilet-clogging incident. And the embarrassing locker moment. And the mountain of homework I'd already been assigned. But overall, I'd navigated my way through my first day at middle school like a real boss. Er, maybe.

✦

The week continued in similar form. Mom kept selecting clothes for me that were almost identical to what I wore in third grade. Anything that featured a loud pattern, a Disney character, or a cartoon was the first thing she reached for. Each morning, I let her choose the clothes and I gritted my teeth, lied by saying I loved them, and got dressed. I sent a picture to Nia, who then picked out a different outfit for me based on what she could remember from my closet, and I put the second outfit in my backpack. Then I changed clothes before school in the same spot as the first day. Since Mom usually picked me up after field hockey practice, I took care to wear my practice clothes and field hockey sneakers so she couldn't tell that I wasn't wearing her outfits. It required a ton of coordination and mental energy, but I would rather put up with that than the embarrassment of wearing her chosen outfits to middle school—or the disappointment of her finding out that I hated the clothing she picked for me.

Each night over dinner, my dad asked me how school was going. As we sat for dinner on Wednesday night, he asked, "Have you started studying? Did you do the reading? How's field hockey? And what other extras are you doing? Can't just study and play a sport—you have to develop some personal interests. Is there a debate team at school?"

"Yes," I said. I did recall seeing a flyer for the debate team in the school library. But I heard mostly seventh and eighth graders join the squad. Besides, wasn't that like fighting in a mock courtroom wearing robes and saying "I object!" to everything? Sounded too intense to me. I don't care for conflict. "I'll keep my options open," I replied. "I was thinking of joining the school paper."

"Mmm," Dad said with furrowed brows. "Well, don't be hasty. Check out some other clubs at the school and figure out what you like. Maybe debate club could be your thing."

By the end of the week, I'd plotted out what looked like a well-rounded semester of classes, sports, and extracurriculars—like the Creeks club, where members went to the creek near school to help maintain the area and feed and take care of the local animals. I like being near the water and I love animals, so this was a nice way of doing my part. Plus, Lee was a member, too.

I'd also calculated how to get to my classes most efficiently after being late for three of them on Wednesday (science, social studies, and gym). Each time I was late, I came up with an even better excuse. (I had to drop off something at the front office; then I had to walk a friend to her class because she'd sprained her ankle and needed someone to carry her backpack; and then the ol' standby: I had to use the restroom.) Each excuse was accepted by my teachers with little drama.

Despite the fibs, I developed a warm rapport with most of my teachers. I didn't think anyone was comfortable around Mrs. Charles, though. She was nice, but she was one of the strictest teachers at the school. And there was a rumor that she gave lots of homework and had an affinity for pop quizzes.

I tried to cram in reading for the social studies lesson, but I couldn't get further than fifty pages into one of the "optional but encouraged" books for the class. When Mr. Brown greeted me before Thursday's class, I thought he was just being nice. "June, right?"

"Yes, sir," I said.

"June Jackson. Things going all right so far?"

"Yes, sir."

"Great!" he said. "Have you done the reading?"

"Yes," I said. *That's true*, I thought. I had done *some* reading, but I was not *done with* the reading. I took my seat before Mr. Brown could ask any more follow-up questions.

Field hockey practices were the smoothest part of the week. Coach asked me what position I was interested in playing, and on Thursday, my name was at the top of the list to be a right wing. My dad was notably proud of me during Thursday's dinner. "All right! My baby's a starter on the field hockey team!" he said. I didn't correct him. I basked in the attention. I just smiled back at him. "You'll be captain by the time you're in eighth grade, watch!"

On Friday afternoon, I walked home with Nia and Olive, who planned to stay over for a bit to talk about the week. My head was spinning from thinking about all the new activities on my schedule. I knew I was going to have to step up to the plate in middle school and start thinking about beefing up my college applications, but my classes and extracurriculars were starting to feel like way too much! This plus the homework and extra reading I'd have to do for school . . . And once field hockey officially began, I wouldn't have much time to hang out with Nia and Olive. I'd have no sense of school-life balance. I might not even have time for Self-Care Sunday! I'd have to sit down with my calendar and figure out how to balance everything! Right then, it seemed like a *lot*.

The three of us reviewed our notes, groaning about science, celebrating Taco Thursday in the cafeteria ("If that happens every Thursday, then I'll make sure never to skip school that day," Nia said), and wondering if Alvin had a girlfriend. "He's eleven, Nia. I doubt he can date," I told her.

"Should we do a study session over the weekend?" Olive suggested. "We could look over our math and science notes. Maybe catch up on the summer reading?"

"Actually, I finished the book Mr. Brown assigned for discussion earlier this week," I lied, "but I'm down. Saturday afternoon? My place?"

"Studying already?" Nia groaned. "It's been a week! What's to study?"

"Fine, come over and hang out and watch us study," I teased. Nia agreed, and the girls gathered up their backpacks to head out. As soon as they'd left, I collapsed on the couch and put my head in my hands.

One week down. I'd managed to make my father happy by playing field hockey, but I was already behind on schoolwork. I was beat. And scared. If I was already this tired after four days of school, how was I going to feel four *weeks* into school, in the middle of field hockey season and classes? And I needed to carve out time for my newspaper stories. Investigative journalism takes a lot of time! I had a vision of myself sitting at my desk, buried under a dozen books, papers scattered around the floor, working in the middle of the night under one small desk lamp, alone, quiet, tired, haggard. I wondered if I would crack under the pressure of sixth grade. I was already looking forward to the next school holiday.

Thankfully, there was one thing on my busy calendar that I knew would provide some much-needed fun and laughs—the annual Featherstone Creek Carnival. But first—one more week of school to survive.

CHAPTER FOUR

I had work up the wazoo. Just like we'd thought, Mrs. Charles had been giving us pop quizzes every few days, and I hadn't been acing them. (On the last one, I'd gotten a B minus. Like allllllmost a C! Dad would be so upset if the third letter of the alphabet appeared on any of my schoolwork!) Social studies required not only studying our textbook but also watching certain news reports via our tablet and YouTube, plus reading a few newspaper articles a week to keep up with current events. English homework was basically assigned by the pound, not the page. How much time in front of screens and papers was I supposed to spend?

Field hockey was just as challenging. On Tuesday, we had our first match, and Coach Dwight put me in the starting lineup. I was nervous, hoping I would score during my first game. My dad was in the stands, too, excitedly cheering me on.

During the first few minutes, I whiffed at an easy pass and let the ball be snapped up by the other team. Thankfully one of our defensive players got it back, but I felt so defeated. My nerves were getting the best of me. I glanced at my dad, and he didn't look too impressed. We still won the match, which was a relief.

Dad found me on the field after the game. "Nice work," he said. "What happened in the first half?"

"Um," I said, nervous to *admit* I was nervous. I wanted him to think I was worthy of my starting position. "In practice I play more defensive positions. Just getting used to all the new formations," I lied.

When we got home, we studied some footage of the game Dad filmed on his iPhone, and he gave me suggestions about what I could do to better position myself. I had no idea he was that skilled at field hockey. My mind raced about formations until I fell asleep that night.

I woke up the next morning and remembered not the field hockey plays I'd just studied but that I forgot to finish my English reading assignment. Why couldn't I just stay on top of everything for one freaking day?!

◆

The annual Featherstone Creek Carnival, a festival slash cookout slash dance party, is the unofficial kickoff to the school year. The downtown square of Featherstone Creek is turned into a magical fall wonderland. All the stores decorate their windows with pumpkins and colored leaves, the restaurants and local chefs sell yummy treats with apple and cinnamon, and the streets are blocked off to traffic so people can walk around freely. Many Featherstone families—like my mom and her aunts and uncles and cousins—have donated money toward the carnival for years. "It's important we support our community. Our philanthropy makes this community what it is," my mother always says.

The entire student body of Featherstone Creek Middle School comes out for the carnival, and parents are either chaperones or work the games, the concession stand, or security. Each year, it gets bigger, better, and brighter. Last year, they got Jazmine Sullivan to perform a half-hour set. It's one of the best things about living in Featherstone Creek.

To say I was excited for this year's festival was an understatement. The last two weeks had been all about making everyone else around me happy—my parents, teachers, even my friends. The festival was the first chance I had to let loose and just be.

On Festival Sunday, Nia, Olive, and I planned to meet

up at the entrance as usual. When we were younger, we used to hold our parents' hands while we walked through the crowd. They took us on the rides, and we begged them to buy us cotton candy. Now that we were in sixth grade, we could run around without our parents' guidance. We were free. Even if just for two hours, and even if just within the town square.

My dad drove into the parking lot located just outside of the main square. We got out of the car and walked toward the entrance of the lot, where we met up with Nia's dad. He gave my dad a fist bump. "What up, man? This parking lot is no joke," he exclaimed.

"Looks like folks came out early this year," my father answered. "Hope they left us some food."

I spotted Nia and her mom across the street before my parents did. "June!" Nia yelled as we walked up to them. "Heyyyy! Hi, Mr. Jackson, Dr. Jackson."

Olive and her family walked up just as I reached into my pocket to see how much money I had on me. "I've arrived!" she said in dramatic fashion. The gang was all together! Finally, no school or drama to distract us—just fun.

My mom came over and put her arm around me. She handed me a twenty-dollar bill. "All right, girls, don't talk to strangers, stay together, and if you get lost, just text one of us. We'll meet at the stage in an hour, okay?" Mom told us.

"Yes, Mom," I answered. Nia and Olive made sure they had enough cash for snacks and some handmade jewelry, and we scooted off toward the concession stand to get ourselves some cotton candy.

Nia wandered over to one of the tall wall displays of fall vegetables and colorful leaves. "I want to be a cool scarecrow for Halloween," she announced. "Like an Alpha Kappa Alpha scarecrow."

"That sounds real specific," I said hesitantly. We were thinking about Halloween already? Geez—I had enough to worry about for the moment, let alone putting together an incredible, showstopping costume!

"I'm going to wear my mom's old sorority sweater, get a bad wig, a hat, striped tights, and carry a broom," Nia said. "Done."

"I have to give this some thought," I said. "Skeleton super-hero maybe? Like Skeleton Wonder Woman? Or Skeleton Leia from *Star Wars*? Ooh, maybe we can do a group theme costume and all be different types of skeleton superheroes!"

"There's an idea," Olive said. "I want to pop in this store, they have those gel pens I like." Olive turned on her heels and disappeared into the local stationery shop. "I'll catch up with you," she shouted over her shoulder.

Nia and I kept walking past kids with their homemade snacks and drinks and parents with their strollers and baby carriers, talking and walking toward various carnival attractions. "So, what's the latest?"

"Where to begin?" I said, letting out a breath. I was relieved she'd asked, honestly—I'd barely had time to see my friends outside of lunch last week, and I was so busy catching up on work while I ate that we'd barely spoken. "School, field hockey, school paper. I want to do a big piece for the paper. Something front page worthy. Something that people are really going to talk about."

"Cool," Nia said. "Like some exposé on the school cafeteria or something?"

"If that's what the people want, I will deliver!"

Nia and I stopped in front of the local ice cream shop on Main Street. We checked our cell phones for texts from our parents or Olive. Nothing from any of them.

"Where's Olive? Taking a long time in that store for some pens," Nia said.

"For real," I said. "Should we wait for her here?"

"I can go back and look for her," Nia volunteered. "Want to wait here?"

"Sure," I said. Nia scooted back the way we'd come. I looked around the square.

I kept walking up the block to admire the decorated storefronts, still in sight of Nia and Olive if they came out of the paper store. I arrived at the corner of Main Street and Elm. I was quite a bit away from most of the action here and turned back toward the rides and stalls, but my eye caught some pink lights framing a building that I hadn't seen before, tucked between two houses. At the front of the building hung a sign: FUN HOUSE, with arrows pointing toward the bright pink front door. I was curious.

I walked toward the fun house and passed some FCMS seventh graders along the way, laughing and giggling as they strolled, and then passed the coffee shop, which was selling something that smelled like cinnamon frosting. As I walked, I had the strangest feeling that someone was following me. But I turned around and recognized no one in particular. And Nia and Olive weren't there, either. Weird . . .

I reached the front door and studied the rest of the house. It had been painted white with pink and purple trim. I'd never seen a house like this in the carnival before. I wondered how they were able to even move it here. I texted the girls to come meet me in front of the fun house and held the phone in my hand for a few minutes, waiting, but they didn't respond.

In retrospect, I should have waited for Nia and Olive, but there was no line to get in, and I was *so* curious.

I figured I'd just check it out, then report back and let them know if it was any fun.

I resolved to go ahead without them and texted them again. **Went in the fun house. Meet me there.**

I tried the handle, and the door breezed open, so I walked through the entrance hallway, where an oversized clown hand attached to the wall stamped my hand as I walked by, and a gate opened and allowed me to pass. There were large warped mirrors lining the walls, some that made my head look twice as large as my body. The hallway was wide and winding and had various bright neon signs flashing from the walls. Upbeat vintage circus music played in the background, but it sounded too fast, like the record had been sped up. It all gave me *Alice in Wonderland* vibes, albeit kinda creepy ones.

My heart started to race as I meandered through, not sure what I would find behind any door. I made my way to what looked like a den. A large bookcase lined one of the walls, and the furniture was oversized. Almost too large, but very cozy-looking. Like if I sat on one of the sofas, I felt like I could disappear straight into the cushions. The music looped repeatedly in the background.

Then I walked into a kitchen, complete with old-school appliances and a worn hardwood floor. But everything was slightly off about it. The walls were bright pink, the refrigerator was a pea-green color, and the table and chairs were larger than normal. Who ate here, giants? I checked the cabinets and the fridge, but they were empty of food. It was like the room had been created by someone who'd seen a human kitchen on TV but had never actually been inside one. I turned to leave the room, and the thought suddenly hit me that I was the only one in the house. The only thing I heard was the sound of my own breath. Suddenly, I heard creaking, like squeaky-shoed footsteps on old floorboards. It seemed as if someone was walking around me, but behind the wall, because I couldn't see anything. The creaking came along the side wall, turned the corner, and continued along to the wall closest to me. The footsteps grew closer until they stopped . . . right in front of me.

Then a plume of dust and pink sparkles seeped upward from underneath the floorboards and swirled around me, like someone had unearthed a gigantic party cracker and let 'er rip. The lighting flickered and went off, plunging the kitchen into darkness. A figure appeared in front of me in a sudden burst and I clenched my eyes shut. I opened them slowly when I felt the air still around me and looked up. A body. A woman's figure. Then a woman's face, with a tiara in her long curly hair. A white sparkly dress with a long train and a bejeweled rhinestone wand. I stood as still as I could. Was this real? What the heck was going on? Was I still in Featherstone Creek? Was I still alive?!

The woman coughed and wheezed as she came into view, then let out a sneeze so exaggerated that she doubled over and dropped her wand. She wiped her nose with the back of her hand and readjusted her tiara atop her head. "Whew!" she said. "Every time I do that, I make such a mess! Oh well . . . Hello, June," the figure said in a pleasant voice. Her smile stretched across her entire face, and her eyes sparkled in the dim light.

I took a step back. "What the . . ." I could barely get words out of my mouth.

"Did I surprise you?" she said, reaching for her wand. She shook it as if she was shaking a remote control with batteries that had very little charge left. "C'mon, this thing! . . . Oops! . . . Oh . . . there we are!" A smooth plume of sparkly fairy dust sprayed from the wand. She turned to me again. "Oh, darling, don't worry, you're safe with me. I'm here to help you! It's a wonder that I was able to keep up with you. You have so much going on

these days between school and your parents and friends. My goodness."

I patted my hands all over my body. I could feel my limbs, so I was still alive, apparently. But was she? Was she a ghost? Was I hallucinating?

"How do you know about my schedule?" I started slowly. "Who are you? Have you been following me?" I asked the . . . woman . . . in front of me.

"My name is Victoria," the figure said. She smiled and bowed her head graciously, the tiara slipping forward again. She pushed it upright.

"Victoria," I repeated. "How in the world did you find me, and why do you look exactly like Tracee Ellis Ross?"

Victoria laughed. "I hear that a lot! Must be the smile. I am, some might say, a guardian angel. But I like to think of myself as more of a fairy godmother."

Did I fall into a Disney movie or something? "A fairy godmother?" I said, dumbfounded. I didn't know whether to believe her, but I decided to play along in case I accidentally angered her by denying that fairy godmothers existed.

"I've got aunts, cousins, a mother, and a housekeeper to look after me. I don't know if I need a fairy godmother. So, thanks but no thanks." I paused, uncertain. "Um, are we still on earth, or have I disappeared off to some other planet?"

Victoria laughed, putting her hand on her chest. "No, darling, we're still here on earth, still here in Featherstone Creek," she said. "But, of course, I have special powers, so for now only you can see and hear me."

"I'll think it's special once I hear what you want," I said with suspicion. My parents always told me not to talk to strangers. And now I'm supposed to trust this strange lady who's telling me that she's a fairy godmother that only I can see? I don't even know her last name! How can I even google her to make sure she's not dangerous?

"Well, as I said, I have been following you for some time," Victoria replied. "And I almost pulled a hamstring chasing you around. You have one busy schedule! But I've also noticed that you seem to be having some trouble expressing your true feelings about your life."

"What are you talking about?" I asked. I thought back to the beginning of school. Was she a teacher? Had she been following me to school? How did she know my name?!

"Just to note a few examples . . ." She paused to take what looked like a small notebook out of the back pocket of her dress, and quickly slipped on a pair of oversized black reading glasses. She read from the pad of paper: "You have trouble telling your mother how you really feel about the clothes she picks out for you. You're having trouble telling your father that you're feeling overwhelmed with schoolwork and field hockey and you have no inter-est in joining the debate team. Or going to Howard, for that matter. You've been lying about liking collard greens for years, you actually hate watching *American Ninja Warrior* with your parents when you could be watching *American Idol*, and deep down your favorite color isn't pink. It's actually teal, but you don't want to admit that to your best friend Nia because you're worried she'll think you're copying her." Victoria whipped off the glasses and slipped them along with the notebook into her back pocket. "So I'm here to help."

"I don't . . . I—how do you know this?" This woman knew all of my deepest, truest feelings. I felt exposed. I felt like I been called out as a liar. But I hadn't been lying to hurt anyone or cause trouble! I'd just . . . selectively told the truth at times. But only to keep people happy and my life as peaceful as possible. *Gasp!* Was she going to tell my parents? What would they do to me when they found out?! If Dad found out I didn't want to go to Howard or be a lawyer, he'd disown me! Mom would get kicked out of Jack and Jill (and my membership would go down the tubes, too). Neither one of them would support me in any way past sixth grade, and I'd be forced to get like three jobs and break all sorts of child employment laws to pay for my own clothes and food! I couldn't let any of this happen. "How can you help me?"

"Let's play a game," Victoria offered.

"What kind of game?" I asked, eyebrows furrowed.

"Two truths and a lie." Victoria had a sparkle in her eye.

I thought about her offer. Things couldn't get any weirder. I was in a crazy fun house with the ghost of Tracee Ellis Ross. Either way, I was going to end this night highly confused and wondering how the heck this Victoria woman found me.

"Why should I tell you more than you already know?" I said. I couldn't give this woman any more evidence than she already had! I resolved to tell her as little as possible, even if I had to lie for the whole game.

"Listen, if I win," Victoria explained, "I will give you a superpower that will help you live your absolute best life, I guarantee. You will feel free, light, and able to live your truth. And if I lose, well, I'll let you go along your merry way, and leave you with just a memory of our meeting."

Yeah, right. Superpowers?! Might as well play along and at least try to make her disappear before she really turned my life upside down.

"All right," I said. "Three things. One, chocolate is my favorite candy. . . ."

"True," she said.

Well, that was an easy one. I tried harder.

"My birthday is my favorite holiday."

"Lie. Christmas is."

Dang it! How did she know? I get more gifts on

Christmas than on my birthday. Have to try a trick response.

"What about, I love field hockey?" I said.

"True-ish," she said. "You're good at it, but you really only play because your dad wants you to."

I stood there silently. She had me after all. She really did know me.

"So, I win," Victoria said. "Now, the superpower I promised you. You ready?"

I braced myself for whatever she was about to present. She was the only "fairy godmother" I'd ever known, and she somehow knew everything about me. Plus, she'd popped up out of nowhere. Maybe it was possible this woman did actually have magical powers. But what could she give me to make my life better? Could I trust her? Did I have a choice? She seemed determined to "help out."

"Not really," I said, "but go ahead. Just don't kill me. I like living on earth."

"I'm not going to kill you, June," Victoria said, laughing. "I'm a fairy godmother, not the Grim Reaper!" I felt better for, like, a nanosecond. "I will, however, give you a superpower you need: the power to tell the truth no matter what."

"Say WHAT?" I replied. Did that mean she'd have control over my thoughts? Over my *mouth*?

"You'll be unable to lie! That way you can express your true feelings at all times to anyone and not feel guilt or pressure. You can do things that make *you* happy, not just things that make others happy."

Telling the truth and nothing but the truth? "And this will be a good thing?"

"Yes, my dear, you just wait," she said, giving herself a twirl. Fairy dust trailed around her body, and she coughed when some of it tickled her throat.

"But what happens if I don't tell the truth?" I asked. "What if I have to lie in certain situations?"

"You won't be able to," Victoria said.

"What do you mean?" I asked. "What if a teacher asks if I did my homework and I didn't? But if I tell the truth, I'll get a bad grade."

"You will have to tell the truth about not doing your homework. You literally will be unable to lie."

I gulped. "What if someone asks me to dance and I don't want to?"

"Then you'll politely decline instead of giving a false excuse," Victoria said.

"What if my mom asks me if I took out the trash, but I didn't, because it smelled awful?"

"Tricky one," Victoria said. "But you'll tell her you didn't take out the trash. You should do what your mother says anyway."

My heart was racing. I thought of all the times I'd smiled when Mom made that gnarly meat loaf with pinto beans (so dry I had to douse a half bottle of ketchup on it) or when Nia told me secrets about boy crushes she had. Or when Lee asked me to go looking for crickets for his pet lizard and I actually picked one up even though I hate bugs, but I did it because it made him happy, and I find it oh-so-cute when he smiles. "What if I spill all my deepest, darkest secrets accidentally to some stranger or to someone I wouldn't dare share my innermost thoughts with?!"

Victoria brought her hands together in front of her heart. "Don't worry, I will be behind you every step of the way to make sure that everything goes okay."

"Goes okay?" I said. Was she joking? "I thought this was going to be a fun way to spend the night at the carnival and kick off my first year at middle school. Instead, I run into a weirdo in a ball gown with a wand who gives me some 'superpower' to only tell the truth and nothing but the truth, no matter who it hurts, and who's gonna follow me around and make sure I don't lie to anybody. I'm supposed to feel good about that? Sorry, lady, but I am *far* from okay right now!"

"Fairy godmother, dear, not 'weirdo in a ball gown with a wand,'" Victoria corrected. "Breathe. Listen, I'm here to help, I promise. The goal of this should be to live truthfully. Tell you what—once you realize that telling the truth is easier than lying, then I'll lift the spell."

What the heck did that mean?! How was I even supposed to achieve that? Lying was *always* easier than telling the truth! Telling the truth hurt my parents, my teachers, my friends. It made them miserable—so it made me miserable. This woman was mistaken if she thought the truth was ever good for anyone. Besides, who knew if this woman even existed? I stood in front of her. No one else was around. No one could see or hear her but me. And even if I did tell anyone about Victoria, *no* one would believe me. If this spell was even real, I was going to have to find a workaround to "prove" to Victoria that I thought the truth was easier—because there was no way I was going to change my mind on this one. Even if she could tell when I was lying . . .

"I'll check in on you from time to time," Victoria said. "And since you're the only one who can see me, you and I can talk without anyone else knowing."

"And what if I lie by mistake?" I said quickly. I had to figure out the rules. If I could figure out the rules of the curse, I could figure out a way to get around them.

"If you happen to get out something less than the truth, I might send a little signal to remind you to stay honest. Just a little reminder that I'm watching."

Victoria waved her wand over my head and a handful of fairy dust fell onto my head and shoulders. I sneezed in reaction. She smiled.

"The power is now within you, June. Remember"—Victoria became transparent as she started to transform into a plume of smoke—"the truth will set you free!"

And in a tornado of dust and sprinkles, my fairy god-mother was gone. I stood there alone, afraid to speak, and wondering what in the world I was going to tell people when they asked me where I'd been for the last twenty minutes.

✦

Dust settled back down to the floorboards of the fun house. I slowly walked backward, retracing the way I'd come, around the corner, through the kitchen, and out the front door. I didn't turn my back on the spot where Victoria had been until I was on the sidewalk.

My breathing grew faster with every step. I jogged up the street toward the corner, where I saw Nia and Olive waiting for me on the sidewalk.

"June, girl, where you been?" Nia said. "Did you really go into the fun house without us? We thought we were going together!"

"Oh no," I said. "I cannot go back in there! It was way too frightening. I—uh—too many clowns," I lied. *Wait . . . I thought I wasn't supposed to be able to lie?* I suddenly felt a powerful itch at my nose, like I really had to sneeze. It borderline felt like my nose was going to explode with snot—the itch was that strong. Was this the signal from Victoria to stay truthful? Was that going to happen every time I lied?! Or was this just a taste of what was to come? Would the reactions get worse? Floods? Locust plagues? "I mean," I added, slightly panicked, "I just can't go back." The itch immediately started to settle.

Nia and Olive looked confused. "Anyway, can we get on the Ferris wheel? Please? Please? Please?" I begged. Anything to not go back to that awful fun house or have to explain myself to Nia and Olive.

"Wow, that bad, huh?" Nia said. "You're sweating."

"I know, right? Ferris wheel?"

Nia and Olive looked at me blankly and shrugged. "Okaaayyyy," they said uncertainly.

I walked ahead of Nia and Olive toward the Ferris wheel, looking down and away from people as much as I could. I wasn't ready to tell them the truth about Victoria. Who knew if they would even believe me! And I certainly wasn't ready to tell the truth and only the truth forever, to everyone. I wasn't sure I *ever* would be. I had to find a way to beat this curse. I had to find a way to trick Victoria into believing I would only tell the truth and nothing but.

CHAPTER FIVE

I tried to enjoy the rest of the carnival. I tried to act normal with Nia and Olive and play carnival games and go on rides. Even after we met our parents at the stage and grabbed some more snacks at the concession stand, I was scared to talk too much, for fear that I might slip up and inadvertently reveal some huge secret. Even pumpkin spice ice cream couldn't brighten my mood. I had a large knot in my stomach, tense from not knowing what might happen if I continued having to tell the truth about everything to everyone for the rest of my truth-telling life.

Nia and Olive tried to chat me up the rest of the night, but they knew something was wrong. "What's up, June?" Olive asked me.

"Nothing, I'm fine!" I said. Was I fine? Was that a lie?

If it was, what would happen? Would I lose my voice? Would there be an earthquake? Or worse? Would someone in my family feel an avalanche of itch in their nose, too? So, I told as much truth as I needed to tell. "That fun house really spooked me."

Olive and Nia looked at me. "See, you should have waited for us," Nia said. "What did you see in there? Now you're going to have nightmares."

"No. It was . . ." I struggled to respond truthfully. "Um. It was more realistic than I thought it would be." That was true for sure.

"Girl, shake it off," Olive said. "Remember, this whole carnival is supposed to be all just for fun! The decorations, the fun house, the rides . . . Maybe get a cup of that homemade apple cider at the concession stand. That'll calm you down."

Just as Olive gave me a reassuring pat on the back, her mom waved to us. "Honey, time to go."

"Ugh, we're always the first to leave a party," Olive moaned. She walked toward her mother with a handful of stuffed animals and handmade crafts she bought from the shops. "I'll see you guys back at school. Text me later." She blew air-kisses to us, then hopped into her family's car. "June, don't worry about that fun house," she shouted from the open window. "Remember, it's all fake! It can't really hurt you. Text me later if you need to take your mind off of it!"

"Thanks," I said to myself as the car drove off. I knew that Olive had no idea how much fantasy had become a reality. She was just trying to be a good friend.

Nia and I turned toward each other. My stomach immediately clenched. She wouldn't let me off the hook as easily as Olive.

"All right, spill it. What happened in there?" Nia said, predictably.

Under normal circumstances, I had trouble telling people about things that really scared me. I was June Jackson, I had it all together! Or at least, people thought I had it together because I never revealed when I was worried about things. But what had just happened to me was too big for me to hold inside.

"I just, I dunno, you know . . . I get scared easily," I said.

"Not like this," Nia said. "You've been petrified ever since you left the fun house. You saw something there. Or someone. And it must have been more than a silly clown or a moving floor. So spill it. What really happened?"

I didn't know what to do. I couldn't lie to her. But telling her the truth might be worse. What if Victoria wanted me to keep her a secret? She never specified! What if I wasn't supposed to tell anyone about the curse? Maybe it didn't matter, because no one could see Victoria except for me? Her "fairy godmother" spell meant I had to either say nothing at all ever again or say everything until I had no friends or family left, and no future or career or anything!

I looked past Nia and saw our parents talking as they walked to us on the sidewalk. I could have stalled to keep from telling Nia anything until our parents caught up with us. But I knew I was going to have to let it out at some point. This spell was too big a secret, too life-changing, for just me to handle on my own. I needed at least one other person to know. At least right now.

My parents were caught up in conversation with Nia's parents and paused before they got any closer to us. I motioned toward an empty bench to the right of Nia and me. "I have to tell you something," I told her. We sat down. Luckily, no one else stood within earshot.

"Yep, you're right. Something happened in the fun house," I began. "No, I don't know if it was real or how to process it. But if I tell you, promise not to tell anybody else."

"I'm your best friend," Nia said. "Of course."

I took a big breath, and everything came out in a rush. "I went into the fun house without you guys, right? I walked into one of the rooms and this dust appeared, and this fairy godmother slash weird lady in a costume was suddenly in front of me. And she told me her name is Victoria and said let's play Two Truths and a Lie. And I lost the game, and she whipped out her magic wand, and then she put a spell on me that makes me only tell the truth about everything. Ev-er-y-thing." I paused finally, out of breath. My shoulders heaved.

Nia looked at me blankly. "Say what?"

I rolled my eyes in frustration. "See, I knew I shouldn't have told you." This was wackadoodle. Who was ever going to believe me?! *I* wouldn't believe me!

I moved to get up, embarrassed as all heck and looking to escape, but Nia pushed me back down on the bench. "Hold on," she said. "Don't run off. I'm just trying to process this. Okay," she said slowly, "so you're saying that a magical fairy godmother slash escaped criminal named Victoria—"

"Yes, exactly," I said, "who looks like Tracee Ellis Ross."

"—who looks like everyone's favorite best friend, met you in the fun house and played Two Truths and a Lie with you. And then put a spell on you so you have to tell the truth. So you can't ever lie." Nia looked skeptical; her lips pursed. I couldn't blame her. I would be, too, if I hadn't lived it!

"Yes," I said. "That's exactly it." I looked around and over my shoulder. I didn't know if I was saying too much about Victoria and if she would suddenly appear and punish me for revealing our encounter. But I felt slightly less scared knowing at least Nia knew what was happening to me. It was the truth, after all.

"So if you can't lie, then you have to tell me the truth about my outfit right now," Nia said, eyebrows raised.

I took a once-over of Nia, who was wearing a baggy T-shirt with leggings and Timberland boots and had her braided hair pulled back into a high ponytail with a headband. "You look like you just stepped out of a rap video from the nineties, but I like it."

"Hmm, okay, bad example," Nia said, skeptical. "Let's really test out this spell of yours. You like Twizzlers, right?"

"Absolutely not! They taste like wax!" I said.

"What about your mom's potato salad?" Nia asked.

"It's too mayonnaise-y!" I replied. It was true. It was always wet, like watery guacamole. It needed less mayo, more potato. And more mustard.

"What about *my* mom's potato salad?" Nia asked.

I clenched my teeth. Nia was not going to like this. "It's flavorless mush," I said. "It's dry and has no seasoning

whatsoever—no salt, no pepper, no Old Bay, no Lawry's seasoning salt. Like, how has this woman been allowed to show up to any family barbecue with that wack potato salad—"

I slapped my hands over my mouth. Oh my gosh, had I really word vomited out how much I hated my best friend's mom's cooking? "Ack! I'm so sorry, please don't tell her!" I grimaced. *How* exactly did Victoria think telling the truth was going to set me free? If this was going to be the result, I should just lock up my mouth and throw away the key for the rest of my life!

"Wow, hating on my mom's potato salad?" Nia said with a side-eye. "Every time you're at my house you rave about it. But you do only eat, like, two bites. . . . Wow." Nia stood and took a few steps back from me. "You really do have a spell over you."

"I know and I'm scared!" I said. "What if I talk to someone and say something that really hurts their feelings?"

"Like you just did with me about my mom?"

"I'm so sorry." I really meant it. I didn't want Nia to be mad at me! And I didn't want things to be awkward when our parents were around, now that she really knew what I thought. God, what if I revealed something bad about Nia to her face? Were my friendships going to survive this curse?

"I know," Nia said. "The spell got you. Plus, I agree with you. That potato salad is pretty mushy."

I laughed with relief but still felt anxious. "But what if I mistakenly blurt out that I have a crush on somebody, or that my mom has bunions or something? Or that I know someone cheated on their quiz at school? I don't want to be a rat! I don't want to tell the family secrets when I'm in math class! I have no idea how powerful the spell really is. What if it prevents me from lying about anything even if lying is the better answer?"

Nia stared at me. "Your mom has bunions? Is that why she never wears flip-flops at the pool?"

"Focus, Nia," I said. "But yeah, kinda!"

Just then our parents walked up to us. "Girls, we have

to get going, it's getting late," my mom said. "Everything all right?"

Ugh. If one more person asked me if I was all right, I would . . . word vomit again. Pretty sure that was both a threat *and* a promise.

"Yes, all good," Nia jumped in right away, saving me the need to lie. "We had fun."

"Did you guys get to see everything you wanted?" Mrs. Shorter said. "Did you go in that fun house up the street? Looked intense."

What do I say, what do I say?! "Yeah, right? Intense." I held my breath, hoping I wouldn't feel a reaction. Was it going to be like this every time I even spoke? This was exhausting!

My mom waved to me. "C'mon, June, grab your things. Did you buy anything while you were walking around?"

"Nope." I hadn't exactly been in the mood to shop after that unexpected visit from my newfound fairy god-mother.

We started walking toward the end of the road and around the corner, to the parking lot where both dads had parked the family cars. The parents went back to their idle chatter. Nia and I continued our conversation.

"I really don't know what you should do," Nia said. "I can't believe you saw a ghost in the fun house and I wasn't there."

"Not a ghost, a fairy godmother."

"Yeah, who looks like Tracee Ellis Ross," Nia said. "Aren't fairy godmothers supposed to be nice and sweet and bring you whatever you've always wanted? Ponies? Prince Charming?"

"She was nice enough, I guess. I'm just scared of what trouble my big mouth might get me into! And who knows what would've happened if you'd been there, too? You might have been put under the spell."

"Or not," said Nia, "since I'm already pretty honest about my feelings toward people. I don't lie to make people feel better. That's not my style. Remember how honest I was about your first day of school outfit."

"True," I said. And while I was slightly embarrassed by her comments that day, she wasn't wrong. Nia had always told me what she really felt, no matter if it might not be what I wanted to hear. But I guess everyone needs a no-filter friend like that in their life. And now, with Victoria's curse, I might have to channel Nia a little bit more in my everyday attitude.

Nia turned to walk toward her mother.

"I'll text you later tonight. We'll figure this out," Nia said.

"Okay," I said. "Thank you. Don't tell anyone!"

"I won't, I won't!"

I walked away from my friend, who looked just as

puzzled about my situation as I felt. I stood up straighter and tried to give off a sense that everything was normal to my parents, hoping no one asked me any questions about the evening. Then I ducked into the car and settled into the back seat.

"Everything all right, June?" Mom asked from the front seat.

"I'm okay," I said. I crossed my fingers and hoped that the car wouldn't suddenly be struck by lightning. Dad pulled out of the parking spot, and we headed back home, leaving the carnival, and the fun house, behind.

✦

I slunk into the house, attempting to avoid my parents as much as possible as we were coming in, and headed straight to my bedroom. I closed the door, flopped onto my bed, and stared at the ceiling, half expecting Victoria to appear out of thin air. I squinted my eyes. Was the ceiling moving? Could I see fairy dust? Nothing. *Phew.*

My phone vibrated in my bag, and I breathed a sigh of relief when I saw a notification from Chloe Lawrence-Johnson, my "best on the west." **Hey girl! What's up?**

Chloe was like an older sister to me—wise, confident, centered—though we were the same age. When I needed a second opinion, or even a first opinion, I went to Chloe.

It's because of her that I appeared to have things in my life handled even when I didn't. Grades, parents, conflict with friends, she's my go-to. And now, when I'd been put under a truth-telling spell thanks to a fairy godmother, Chloe was the one voice of reason I desperately needed to hear.

> **JUNE:** Thank goodness, it's you. I have to tell you something super, ultra-top secret. But you cannot tell a soul. Not your mother, not your diary. No one. Okay?

Chloe FaceTimed me immediately and I picked up. "Daaannng," she said. "What happened?"

I told Chloe the whole story. Victoria. Spell. Truth. Life over.

"Girl. This is heavy," Chloe said.

"I know!"

"Is Victoria there?" Chloe asked.

"No." I looked around the room. I didn't see her. "But I also get the feeling she won't always announce herself before she appears."

"Hmm, well. I have an idea," Chloe said. "Victoria said you always have to tell the truth—but not to a certain person. You could tell the truth under your breath or talk to yourself, and you could be fine, right?"

Chloe had a fair point. Could that work? "But then I'll look weird if I'm talking to myself everywhere."

"Maybe if you whisper?" Chloe said.

"My lips would still be moving."

I sighed and looked at my desk. I looked at my computer. Then, an idea came to me.

"Wait," I said. "I could write down the truth! Maybe if I write it down somewhere, I can get around the spell."

"A journal," Chloe responded.

"Right!" But did I want a diary? Something my mom could find under my pillow? Or Victoria could find? I needed something more secret. Something only I could access. "Maybe a blog?"

"Yeah, that could work. Make it password protected!"

"Yaasss, that's better!"

I jumped straight to my computer and pulled up the WordPress home page. I paused briefly to think of a title for the blog. June Tells It All? Nah. Nothing but June's Truth? Eh. Honest June? Ooh, catchy. And true. And available. I typed it in and hit Publish.

Instantly, I had created a secret place for my private truths. Now if there was anything that I was too scared to say out loud, I could type it here. It would hopefully satisfy Victoria's spell, and I didn't have to worry about letting out secrets and thoughts I didn't want to share.

"Perfect! The truth will always live here," I said.

"And with me!" Chloe said. "You can't lie to your best friend."

I sat back in my seat and exhaled. My blog could be my secret weapon against Victoria's spell! Anything I was too scared to reveal, any truths I didn't want spoken out loud, I could type them down. This would definitely come in handy during class, especially when I'm supposed to seem interested in social studies when I'm actually bored to tears.

I smiled to myself, proud of my new scheme. As I glanced around my room, my eyes drifted to a corner underneath the window. There, in a tidy pile near my nightstand, was sparkly dust, twinkling under the light of the night sky streaming in from the window. Luisa, our housekeeper, cleaned my room every other day, and there was no way she would have missed this amount of dust. As I stared, a small amount of the dust seemed to rise up and float a few inches in the air, dance around, and gently settle back to the pile. I realized instantly it wasn't dust. It was something much more magical.

It was Victoria, monitoring my every truth-telling, or *attempt* at truth-telling, move.

HONEST June

CONFESSION #1:

Of all the fun houses in all the towns in all the world, how did this Victoria fairy godmother find ME? Okay, I haven't always been as honest as I could be with people about my feelings. But it was for the greater good of peace and harmony in the world—or at least, *my* world! My parents think I'm great, my friends think I'm cool, and so far my teachers think I'm smart—how is truth going to help me live a better life? What if this Victoria has some other motive besides "helping" me, like learning about all my deepest darkest secrets so she can expose my information to her tribe of godmommies in never-never land? So they can . . . I don't know . . . expand their evil empire!

Or what if Victoria's right? What if it actually is easier to tell the truth?

Yeah, right!

CHAPTER SIX

I just had to make it through Monday morning—and then a full day of school—without lying. Then I could devote some time to figuring out how to get out of this mess! As soon as I could show Victoria that I could tell the truth for a whole day, I could prove to her that I thought it was easier to tell the truth than lie. And then she'd have to apologize and take back the curse—right?

I decided my main strategy for getting through the day was to *not* talk. I'd avoid conversation with people, so I didn't have to say anything at all! Which was hard in itself—how was I supposed to be my charming, funny, intelligent self at school by saying nothing? If I couldn't fix this by tomorrow, how was I going to play field hockey and say nothing to my teammates? Or answer when teachers called on me in class? I didn't even want to eat in the cafeteria so I couldn't accidentally tell the lunch ladies the truth about that mystery Jell-O they serve every day—that it's no mystery, it's just plain nasty.

Picking out my clothes was my first big test. I dreaded waking up for the morning. If my mom picked out something I didn't like, I'd have to somehow stop myself from telling her what I really thought about her picking out my clothes from OshKosh B'gosh.

But I got lucky. Mom had to go to the hospital for a delivery. She left a note for me in my bathroom that said, "Have early appointments scheduled every morning this week, so I'll miss you in the mornings. I left lunch for you today, in case you don't want to buy lunch at school. I'll see you at home tonight. Love you!"

Yessssss! Double score!

I went to my closet and picked out my favorite yellow dress with a denim jacket—no prints, no Disney characters—and my Nikes. Phew! One potential disaster avoided so far.

I bounded downstairs and almost bumped into Dad, who was packing up his briefcase to head to the office. "Morning, sweetheart, all good?" he said.

Was it? I paused. "Yeah," I said, scared to say much more.

He looked at me. "You finish your homework?"

That I had. "Yes."

"You need a ride to school?"

"No, I'm going to walk with Nia and Olive."

He looked at my outfit from head to toe. "Did Mom pick that out?"

I shuddered. I wanted to say yes so he wouldn't keep asking me questions. But my lips wouldn't form the word. My nose began to itch, as if I was allergic to lying. A tell-tale, or tell-truth, itch—or a warning from Victoria to tell the truth! "No," I said. I shuddered. *Oh please, oh please don't ask any more questions!*

He looked at my dress once more. Then he nodded.

"Cute," he remarked, then gave me a kiss on the cheek. "I'll see you later. Be good in school."

I let out a huge sigh of relief as soon as he stepped out the door and poured myself a bowl of Honey Oats. I ate quickly, then dropped my bowl in the sink, grabbed my backpack, and hustled to the end of the driveway where I could wait for Nia and Olive.

It was another warm fall day in Featherstone Creek. Birds were chirping. The sun felt warm but not too hot. We could wear dresses without tights or leggings here until at least mid-November without feeling cold.

Nia and Olive were chatting as they walked toward my driveway. "Hey, girl!" Nia said. "Like the outfit!"

"Thanks," I said. "Mom was at work already, so I picked this out myself."

"That's good. Then you didn't have to lie about liking whatever she chose for you."

"Exactly."

Olive looked at me. "So, you get over that fun-house scare yet?"

I looked at her, afraid to answer again. So far this "keeping silent" plan was harder than I thought it was going to be. Nia jumped in and did the talking for me. "She's good."

I kept my mouth shut while we walked to school. I held my breath as we walked into the main entrance, and hoped Victoria wasn't watching me, even though she said she would be. Every day. No matter what.

I avoided people as much as possible throughout the day. Whenever kids wanted to chat, like when Rachelle asked the class if they liked her new tie-dyed shirt, I kept my head low and pretended not to listen, fighting the urge to sneeze. (For the record, Rachelle, it's fine. Not something I would buy, but not horrible. She didn't need to hear that, though.)

I typed any truths I was nervous I might accidentally reveal in the notes app of my school tablet to put into my blog later that day. Like when Lee walked into science class and he looked really cute in his polo shirt and khakis and I had to fight not to compliment him. I didn't want him—or anyone—to know I thought he was cute. Or adorable. Or perhaps my future husband. I typed into my notes: Lee looks really cute today. I like how his blue shirt highlights his skin. And his smile. 🖤 😘

Then I tripped and fell over my own clumsy feet while walking to my locker between science and social studies classes, and fell in between Curtis James, an eighth grader on the football team, and his pal Lorenzo Tate. Curtis helped me up, but he thought Lorenzo had knocked me down. "Dude, watch where you're going! Ladies are passing by."

"I didn't push her!" he said.

I was so embarrassed after falling that I stood up and

shuffled off as quickly as possible and was immediately hit with a gigantic fairy-dust-induced sneeze attack. I felt bad that Lorenzo took the blame for my fall, so I typed the real story into my secret blog in the bathroom afterward:

CONFESSION #2:

Falling onto one of the 8th-grade football players was just mortifying! It wasn't Lorenzo Tate's fault I fell into Curtis James. It was my own two clumsy feet. But I was so embarrassed, I slunk off before I could stumble even further over my own words to explain. I definitely looked awkward as heck, and I betcha anyone who saw me is laughing at me now. But if I could pretend Lorenzo tripped me, at least I could save myself from further humiliation!

I met up with Nia and Olive at lunch, where I mostly kept my mouth shut, hand wrapped around a package of tissues I kept in my backpack in case I sneezed, because I didn't want to tell the truth. I didn't want to expose myself to a potential situation where I would have to speak the truth, and nothing but the truth.

That's why I was especially relieved to head off to my extracurriculars for the day. The one place where the truth wouldn't get me into trouble for sure was while I was working on the school newspaper. Any story I wrote had to be the truth, or it couldn't be printed. And I had to be honest about any work I did on those stories. Here, I felt safe.

The newspaper office was a large room with several computers, stacks of magazines and newspapers, and plenty of couches and chairs for students to gather and chat. Framed oversized copies of past issues hung on the wall, along with group photos of each year's newspaper staff.

Ms. April West was the faculty advisor for the school paper. She was an eighth-grade English teacher and one of the younger teachers on campus. She had come to FCMS right out of grad school, and her entire family was from Featherstone Creek. A lot of kids looked at Ms. West like a big sister in some ways—she had cool clothes and fun shoes, and she even wore big hoop earrings at times—

though usually on Fridays. She talked to students who worked on the paper like they were her peers, not just her students. I heard she'd often bring in interesting articles she'd read from other newspapers and websites to show students story ideas and examples of good writing. And when she assigned stories, she thought about each student's interests and asked them to write what they know. Since I was on the field hockey team, at our first newspaper meeting on Monday afternoon, she'd given me a story about the budgets for the athletic teams. I'd heard a rumor that the girls' teams received less money than the boys' teams, and I asked to investigate it.

"Why don't you ask some coaches and the athletic director and see if that's true? Get the facts first, June," Ms. West said. "Then see how other student athletes might feel about it."

I managed to set up a quick meeting with the athletic director, Mr. James, before field hockey practice the next day to ask him about it. He told me that it was the school's policy not to talk about specific numbers but that the amounts were mostly in line with the number of girls playing sports compared to the number of boys. As in, more boys playing sports equaled more money. Hmm.

I also reached out to both the football coach and the cheerleading coach and asked my coach, Ms. Dwight. "I will only say that the more funds we get, the more equipment and clothing we can provide to help keep the girls safe and happy," Ms. Dwight told me right before practice. "If the school doesn't value female athletes' safety and happiness as much as the male athletes', then that's disappointing."

I agreed with her. After I finished practice that afternoon, I came home and sent out a few more emails asking for details. And after some more digging, it turned out the girls' teams got a third less in funding than what the boys' teams got. That was so unfair! But I couldn't say that in the story; this wasn't meant to be an opinion piece, so I wasn't allowed to write about any of my own feelings. How the heck was I going to write an article about just the facts when I felt so strongly that this was wrong?!

As I sat at my desk, my nose suddenly had an itch that burned all the way down to my stomach. It was like the words were rushing up my throat. If I accidentally burst out with these feelings, it was going to make a lot of people upset—and seriously jeopardize Ms. West's trust in me that I could report the facts without giving the audience my feelings. I could get kicked off the paper! What to do?

Oooooh, secret blog! I suddenly remembered. Duh! I could write my personal feelings about the differences there so I could focus on only reporting the straight facts in the story.

I pulled up the website and felt my feelings flow freely from my fingertips:

CONFESSION #3:

If it's true that the girls' sports teams at FCMS don't get as much money for their teams as the boys' sports teams, then SMH. It's straight shady. It's not fair! I think girl athletes should protest! Walk off the field! Sit out during games! March and hold sit-ins until we get what we deserve!

I exhaled the air out of my lungs, letting loose any frustration that had built up over my research for the story. It felt good to express myself, and in the end, I got out my true feelings without hurting anyone. *Ha! This blog thing is really genius!*

Now all I had to do was find the time to write the article between field hockey practice and homework. Oh, and figure out how to overturn this darn truth curse and get my free will back from Victoria. No sweat, right?

HONEST June

CONFESSION #4:

I survived a whole two days under Victoria's spell. I can't say life is that much better than it was before—it's just been worse all around! My survival tactic of saying as little as possible and using the secret blog to release the things I'm too nervous to say out loud is working out so far. But I'm exhausted—it's a lot of work to tell the truth, or only tell the truths I want people to hear! I'm not going to be able to do this for much longer without losing my mind. But first I have to somehow prove to Victoria that I actually want to tell the truth. Only then will I finally have a chance of overturning this spell.

CHAPTER SEVEN

It was eerily quiet in my room late Thursday night. I'd stayed up late to study and continue working on my article, and it was way past my bedtime. I couldn't even hear the hum of the overhead fan whirring around. Then I heard a slow hiss, like sand moving in an hourglass. It got louder. My room got foggy with what looked like stardust. Then a large gust of dust gathered in the middle of my room, spinning quickly until a woman's body appeared. Good ol' Victoria.

She coughed loudly, then smoothed the dust off her dress. "Goodness, this dust does get on *everything*. Hi, June!"

"You just pop up out of nowhere, huh?" I said to her.

"Part of my superpowers as a fairy godmother," she

said, bowing in front of me, her tiara falling off her head and onto the floor.

"What have I done wrong now?"

"Oh my dear," Victoria said, picking up the tiara and placing it back on her head. It tilted to one side. "I was just going to compliment you on how well you're managing so far."

"On how well I'm managing?" I said, crossing my arms. She obviously hadn't been watching me too closely, or else she would have seen me working overtime to not speak for fear I would expose some gnarly things about myself! "I have never worked so hard to keep my mouth shut in all my life."

"But that's no way to live life, darling. Remember, this is about *telling* the truth," Victoria said.

I felt anxious just thinking about how much longer I'd have to survive with this spell. Who might get hurt? Who might find out some deep dark secret about me and use it as blackmail? "Look, any chance you can lift this blessed curse early?" I begged Victoria. "I'm on the school paper! Every week I have to report the truth to help my fellow students stay informed about current events. Doesn't that count for something?"

"No, my dear," Victoria said. "You need to prove you can choose to tell the truth—your *own* truths, not just the truth about history or current events—over lying. You can't just grin and bear it, and you can't just say nothing.

You need to prove that even when the truth hurts, you tell it anyway."

I slumped my shoulders and rolled my head toward the floor. "What is this really going to do for me?" I asked.

Victoria waved her magic wand over my head and fairy dust fell on my shoulders. "More than you know, my dear. Really, give the truth a try."

The mythical woman waved her wand in a circle, twirling at the same time, and a cloud of fairy dust surrounded her. The cloud turned into a funnel, swirling around until it seemed to erase her from my sight. The dust fell into a pile in front of my desk. I bit my tongue as I went to the broom closet and cleaned up Victoria's mess.

◆

"All right, ladies," Ms. Dwight said as we lined up for warm-ups on Friday afternoon. I had just made it to the line when she blew her whistle. I'd gone to bed an hour past my bedtime the past three nights just so I could keep working on my article, and I was completely wiped out.

"Knees up, knees up!" Coach yelled. Getting my knees up to my chest felt like lifting heavy bags of flour. These didn't seem so hard during tryouts!

I looked over at Coach, who was sitting in the bleachers with a teacher and some new girl I didn't recognize before. The girl was tall, with long hair and clear skin. Had to be at least a seventh grader—maybe even an eighth grader. I kept warming up. Next was skips with hip openers. Knee up, knee out, knee up, knee out.

Then we moved on to sprints, which were the last thing I was in the mood for. I moved as fast as my legs would carry me, which was still faster than most of the team. After two lengths up and down the field, Coach Dwight blew her whistle. "Girls, hustle up. I have an announcement."

We gathered in front of Coach on the sideline, where she stood next to the new girl.

"Girls, I want to introduce you to our newest teammate, Blake Williams. She just transferred to FCMS from the East Coast. Welcome, Blake. Blake's in sixth grade and played field hockey in Boston at her old school."

Blake kept smiling as she looked at all of us. She was prettier the longer I looked at her.

"Blake did a tryout for us over the last few days and is amazing. I think she'll make a great forward. Make her feel welcome, girls. Blake, make sure to ask anything you need to know, okay?"

"Yes, Ms. Dwight," Blake answered in a soft voice. She moved gracefully toward the line.

"All right, girls, let's get into our scrimmage teams and go for a round. I'll put Blake on Kenya's team. Blake and June, you're both on offense."

I grabbed my gear and got ready for the scrimmage. Blake walked slowly toward the gear bags packed with hockey sticks, protective pads, and spare helmets. Other girls introduced themselves as she got ready to take the field.

Blake turned and made eye contact with me. I sprang forward to introduce myself.

"Hi, I'm June."

"Nice to meet you," she said.

"When did you get here?"

"I started today officially. I came after third period. I visited during the first day of school and then flew back home to pack and move with my parents. And today we had to finish up some things in the main office first."

Ah, this was probably who Nia was referring to on the

first day of school. "Gotcha. Well, welcome. We're happy to have you on the team. Let's play!"

We got into formation for the scrimmage. Coach blew the whistle and the game began. Blake was fast. Her footwork was on point, too. Like, she'd certainly played club hockey at least. Kenya passed me the ball and I ran to the right, then left, then, *shloooop!* . . . The whistle blew. Goal!

"Nice one!" Kenya said to me as I ran by. We scored two more goals over the other team before the end of practice.

Blake and I talked between drills. "I heard that people in Boston have funny accents," I blurted out, because that was honestly on my mind ever since I heard her speak.

"Not all of us, and I grew up all over the East Coast— Boston, New Jersey—so maybe I never kept any specific accent. We were last in Massachusetts, outside of Boston," Blake said. "We transferred here for my dad's job."

"Cool. What does your dad do?"

"He's a lawyer at a firm called something like Thurston Smith something. A bunch of names."

"Get out!" I squealed. "That's my dad's firm. He's the Jackson in Thurston Jackson Shorter Smith."

"Oh really! What a coincidence! Dads as lawyers. Means we can never win an argument."

"That is so true." I laughed. Blake was easy to get along with, as far as I could tell. Maybe field hockey could be more than something I just did because my dad wanted me to. Maybe it could be fun. Fun with Blake.

After a few more plays, we finished up practice. I was sweaty and tired, but Blake looked like she'd barely broken a sweat. "Where do you live? Like, where is your new place?"

"I'm just around the corner, on Cedar Street." Blake said.

"That's literally around the corner from where I live! I'm on Houston."

"Really? Maybe we can hang out sometime."

"Yeah, that would be so fun!" I said enthusiastically, and internally cringed. So much for playing it cool.

"Great," Blake said, grabbing her gear and waving. "It was fun chatting! I'll see you at practice next week."

✦

I'd made it through nearly a week without telling a lie. I had never put so much thought into every word that came out of my mouth before. I was careful to tell the truth, but only truths I wanted people to hear. The rest were hidden safely on my blog. But I had to figure out a way out of this spell—and quick! Especially since I had so much to hide—I got a C plus on my latest math quiz. Like, barely above average! I had to turn my grade around before my parents found out. And if I didn't catch up on both my social studies and my English lit reading, those grades were about to tank as well.

After practice, Nia and Olive met me by the main school entrance so we could walk home together to celebrate the start of the weekend. Olive had stayed late for orchestra practice and Nia had had a meeting about basketball tryouts, though their season started later in the school year.

"Have you guys seen the new girl at school? Blake Williams?" I said to the girls. "Nia, I think that's the girl you saw on the first day of school."

"Tall girl?" Nia asked.

"Yes, and super good at field hockey. I just met her today. And guess what? Her dad works at our dads' firm. She's originally from Boston."

"Oh, right! Now this is all coming together," Nia said. "Dad did mention that there was a new guy coming to town. I kinda remember this conversation between my mom and my dad at the dinner table."

"Is she cool?" Olive asked.

"Yes, she's super cool," I gushed. It was true. "She lives around the corner from us. And she's traveled all over the country. And she's got great skin—like, it *glows*. And she's, like, really good at field hockey."

"Uh-huh," Nia said slowly. I realized I had said a lot

of words in a row without taking a breath, but I couldn't stop myself from barreling on anyway.

"Anyway, I think that she's super cool, and, like, her voice is just . . . like listening to the radio."

"Really, June?" Nia said, tilting her head to the side, crossing her arms, and pausing our walk to rock back on one hip. "You have a crush on this new Blakie Blake? I haven't heard you say so much about anything since that day you tried the chocolate chip ice cream at Dips."

So I *had* said too much! And now Nia was making me feel bad about thinking Blake was cool. See, when inner dialogue became outer dialogue, people judged you! "I'm just saying she's cool, and I'm sure you guys would like her, too."

"I'm sure she was cool," Olive said. "We should hang out at some point, particularly if she lives around the corner."

"No new friends," Nia said. I was shocked at her words and shook my head in surprise. This was the girl that had the phone number of every Featherstone Creek kid under fourteen in her phone. Nia never did anything alone—if she wasn't hanging out with me, she was with Olive. Why couldn't she make room for one more friend?

"What is this, a mafia?" Olive asked, eyebrows shooting sky-high.

"You know what I mean. Listen, I like people and all,

but I trust you two with my deepest secrets, and I don't know if I can welcome in any new members to my circle."

"Your circle is half of the entire school," Olive retorted. "Didn't you invite three hundred people to your birthday party and tell your dad all of them were very close friends?"

"Well, they were," Nia said, "and now I have too many friends. And that's why I have to close the circle. Sorry, Blake."

"That's stupid," I said sharply. More sharply than I'd expected. "What's the big deal?"

"You barely know her," Nia said.

"But we're getting to know her—that's why we would invite her over," Olive said.

"Well, I don't think I have the time these days, and it doesn't sound like you two do, either," Nia spat back.

My nose began to itch uncontrollably, and I felt a rush of words coming from my belly to my mouth, a rush of words I instantly wished I wouldn't have said out loud, but I couldn't stop the word vomit. "What it sounds like to me," I said, "is that you are a little bit jealous of Miss Blake. Perhaps Blake is too perfect and too pretty for you."

I had never said anything so mean to my best friend before. But Nia was acting so weird and jealous about Blake! I couldn't stop myself from pointing it out. . . .

"That is *so* not true," Nia said, whipping her head back.

"I barely saw her. And, no, I'm not jealous of a new girl. I'm all for new blood in Featherstone Creek."

I couldn't stop myself from coming for Nia once more. "You sure about that, Nia?"

Olive smiled at us and held her hands out between us like a referee. "Well then, let's invite Blake to a study day. Let's all get together and get to know her better."

"All right, fine," Nia said with exasperation. "If you two want to hang out with her soooo badly . . ."

I felt another truth explosion about to erupt from my belly. Before I could catch myself, something came out of me I never thought I'd ever say to my best friend since the womb. "Maybe you're jealous that I have friends *other* than you!"

I was stunned. The truth had come flying out of me like a caged bird. And I felt *horrible* about it.

Nia looked at me, her mouth open. "Girl, really?" she said. I was mortified at myself. Nia had been acting catty, that was true. It wasn't the first time, and it wouldn't be the last. But I had *never* called her out on it—not even when she was at her meanest. What I had said was petty and cruel. If telling the truth all the time meant that I was going to lose Nia in the process, then Victoria had to see she wasn't here to help me at all. Instead, she was *ruining my life.*

Nia backed away from Olive and me. "I'll see you later, Olive," she said, turning to cross the street away from us.

Olive gave me one last sad look and turned to walk to her own house. I stood, mouth gaping, as my friends walked away. I desperately wanted to take back my last sentence, but it was too late. I'd deeply hurt my best friends' feelings. The truth had cracked one of the longest and closest friendships of my life. And I was less than a week into Victoria's spell.

HONEST June

CONFESSION #5:

I got into a stupid fight with my best friend today. Over another girl. How silly is that? Nia and I have been best friends since forever and now she's jealous of Blake Williams? Why? Because she's pretty? And nice? And lives in one of the biggest houses in our subdivision? Come on, what's not to like?

Nia has always been so quick to shoot off an opinion about people, like the way she ragged on Kenya after the Christmas talent showcase last year, telling everyone she couldn't dance. And Kenya has been studying tap for years.

Nia, I love you, but, dang, girl, you are petty with a capital *P*.

CHAPTER EIGHT

I was studying at my desk in my room later that night. Well, *trying* to study. My mind was thinking about Nia, about Blake, and about what Nia could possibly not like about Blake. Then, I felt the air shift. A cold whiff of air blew around my shoulders. A plume of dust appeared in front of me. Oh no. I had company.

I turned toward the middle of my room. The tornado of dust swirled around and got thicker and tighter until the shape of Victoria appeared right in front of me. "Hello, my dear," she said. "Just checking in! Each day you seem to be getting along under the spell of truth."

"Barely!" I said incredulously.

Victoria sat on my bed. "I admit, I did see that instance of you calling out Nia for being jealous."

"Yeah," I scoffed. "Thanks to you, words just came spilling out. I hope the truth hasn't cost me a friendship."

"But that's what you were truly feeling, right?" Victoria said. "Most of the time our true feelings come out so that we can free ourselves from burden, not so that we can please other people."

"Maybe I can pick and choose when I have to tap into my so-called honesty? Like if you know I would hurt myself, or if I saw someone doing something illegal, or if I thought a friend needed my advice on a life-changing problem, then I could be honest?"

"Sorry, my dear, the spell doesn't work that way," Victoria said, snapping her fingers for effect. A bit of fairy dust floated from her fingertips. "It's designed so that you tell the truth, the whole truth, anytime and anywhere."

I groaned. There had to be some way I could undo this spell. Like clicking my heels three times, or throwing holy water at a mirror in the dark, or giving one of my first Cabbage Patch dolls to a child in need or something!

"This is for your own good!" Victoria said, reacting at the look of desperation on my face. "Look, I'm here as your fairy godmother—you're in my charge. It's my job to make sure you don't get into harm's way from the truth telling. I promise. Now, carry on as you were. You're doing great—but you're not ready to let go of the spell just yet!"

"But wait!" I shouted. "I swear it's easier for me to tell the truth now! I learned my lesson! You can undo the curse!" I said with a sneeze. But it was too late. As Victoria began to spin, a plume of sprinkles and stardust created a tornado around her until she disappeared into thin air once again, leaving not one speck of dust in her wake. I turned back to my desk. All that was left in front of me was a mound of homework to tackle.

✦

I sent a text to Chloe after I finished up an assignment.

> **JUNE:** Hey girl. I may have to move in with you.

CHLOE: What's happening?

> **JUNE:** This honesty spell is not working in my favor. I got into a huge fight with Nia because I told her I thought she was jealous of this new girl in town, Blake.

CHLOE: Oof.

> **JUNE:** And I'm drowning under all this homework. Plus the newspaper. Plus field hockey. I haven't gone to bed before midnight all week.

CHLOE: Can you tell your parents or teachers you're honestly overwhelmed and you could use a break?

JUNE: No! Do you really think Howard Dad will allow his daughter to "take a break"? No. More is more. My whole life is programmed around "that's how you get into Howard."

CHLOE: Well, you're not at Howard right now. And you have every right to take your foot off the gas. Which assignment is most urgent?

JUNE: This story for the school newspaper is due Wednesday morning.

CHLOE: So do that first. Sentence by sentence, paragraph by paragraph. Then deal with what's after that.

JUNE: Yeah, I guess. And what do I do about Nia?

CHLOE: She'll come around. Text me later.

◆

I spent all weekend writing the article for the paper and stayed up way past bedtime Tuesday night to get it ready to go for Wednesday morning. I typed until my eyeballs burned and my butt fell asleep in my chair, but I had to finish. At some point I fell asleep in my clothes, mid-sentence, because I had typed the letter G approximately 250 times when my finger stalled on the keyboard. Thankfully, it was at the end of the article. I deleted the Gs and hit send at about 12:30 a.m. Then I crawled into bed, too tired to even wash my face, and fell asleep instantly.

Wednesday morning came way too early. My alarm went off, but I didn't hear it, and Dad had to yell my full name (yikes!) for me to stir awake. I slowly rose out of bed and got ready for school. Everything seemed super hazy through sleepy eyes. Dang, my face looked tired. Those bags under my eyes. Pass the cucumber slices. Maybe Mom left some coffee in the coffeepot? She'd be

angry if she knew I drank any. Maybe a few Diet Cokes could help?

Mom left early for the hospital again, so I was free to pick out my own clothes. I went with a blue striped dress that came down to my knees and grabbed a gray sweater and tied it around my waist in case I got too cold. I slid on a pair of Converse and headed downstairs for breakfast.

I searched for the sugariest cereal in the house, hoping to give myself an energy boost before heading to school. There, in the back of the cupboard, was a six-month-old box of Frozen Ritas flakes that I had begged Mom to buy and had eaten maybe two bowls of before she lectured me about the amount of sugar included in each serving.

I thought Mom had thrown it out, but thankfully she'd only hidden it. Today was an emergency, though. I poured a bowl for myself, then splashed on a river of almond milk and dug in.

"I thought Mom threw that stuff out," Dad said as he walked in to grab his keys.

"I thought so, too." This was true. "Luckily, she didn't."

I wolfed down the cereal and rushed to grab my book bag. My phone vibrated with a text notification from Nia that she was waiting outside to walk to school.

> **JUNE:** Oh, I didn't think you wanted to walk with me.

> **NIA:** Why? Because of Blake?
> Girl, please. I don't want to be late.

Through the window, I could see Nia talking to Olive, smiling and waving her hands as if she was telling some good gossip. Nia seemed to be in a good mood. Maybe we wouldn't have to talk about the Blake thing.

"Hey," Nia said as I walked up. "You good?"

"Yeah, just tired."

"Late night?"

"I had this story for the school paper due. And home-work."

"Right, like our math quiz today," Olive said.

My head whipped around. "What math quiz?"

"The one Mrs. Charles said at the end of Monday's class we're having today. Did you forget to study?"

Oh no. "Dang it! I didn't even crack open my math books this week!"

"I thought you said you studied."

"I studied everything but math," I said.

"Let's chat about whatever we can in the time we have until we get to school," Nia said.

I could not believe I had let this happen. I had *never* not studied for a test. I always wrote in my planner when quizzes were coming up. I always looked at my notes the same day after class just to make sure I at least *looked* at the work, just in case there *did* happen to be a pop quiz the next day—I was that paranoid! But between school, all my after-school activities, and my mind in overdrive trying to figure out how to get out from under this spell, I dropped the ball. I'd never been so off of my academic game.

I took out my notes and began reviewing whatever I could from the last few lessons on the walk to school. Olive repeated formulas to me while Nia shouted out some example equations. But I knew deep down that ten minutes wouldn't be enough for me to get a good grade on the quiz. We walked through the main entrance. I kept looking at my notes as I walked to my locker, unloaded a few books, then continued on to class, walking as slowly as I could to get in as much precious study time as possible.

I prayed that Mrs. Charles had called out sick and that a substitute teacher would be sitting at her desk, but no such luck. Mrs. Charles was waiting, looking sharp and healthy, the quizzes stacked in a nice, neat pile on her desk. I sat at my usual desk, slumped in the seat. "I am honestly terrified," I whispered to myself as I mentally prepped to face my doom.

◆

And there it was. The next day, I received my grade from Mrs. Charles on our quiz, in a bold red capital letter, like a brand or a stamp. I had never seen that letter on top of any schoolwork I'd ever done, but here it was, the one, the only:

The dreaded C minus.

"Oh. My. Goodness," I said, my heart breaking. Olive looked over my shoulder.

"It could have been worse," Olive encouraged. "It could have been a D minus."

But to my parents, my father especially, there was no worse. If it's not an A, it might as well be an F. And *this*, this disgrace of a grade, was guaranteed to generate smoke from his ears and make those large eyebrows scrunch up so hard that they touch in the middle of his forehead. And thanks to my newfound superpower, or unfortunate ability, I would inevitably end up telling my parents about it, even if I tried to conceal it. And it wouldn't be pretty. But they were bound to ask about it; last night at the dinner table, when they asked me what I'd done that day, I blurted out that I took a math quiz. And what would I say now?

I couldn't possibly tell the truth. The consequences—disappointing my parents, my father and those eyebrows, punishment!—were too dire.

So maybe I wouldn't tell them at all.

What if I could avoid seeing them at all after school? Could I go to bed at, like, 5:00 p.m.? Nah, they'd never believe I was that tired. Could I eat my dinner in my room, using the excuse that I had too much homework to come down for a proper meal? That was the truth! But then they'd come in to kiss me good night, and they'd ask questions. Could I fake being asleep then? Drat!

There were no good options for me here, but I couldn't

tell them the truth without being kicked out of the family permanently. Just like at school, I was just going to have to avoid talking to them entirely. Saying nothing isn't lying.

Right?

CHAPTER NINE

✦✦
✦

Not only is Blake an amazing field hockey player, but also she's a math whiz. She scored ninety-five percent on our math quiz. My math grade was currently twenty points lower than hers. *Average.* My father does not like average. He does not know the word *average.* Me bringing home a C minus was grounds for being kicked out of the Jackson family and having to change my last name permanently. Thankfully he didn't know. Yet.

I found Blake at field hockey practice that afternoon and confessed that I needed to study extra hard in math. "Why don't we study together sometime?" she offered. "We studied some of these theorems in my old school."

"That would be amazing," I said. "Do you want to come over after school one day? Maybe even tonight?"

"Sounds great," she said. "I'd love a study buddy."

Me too, I thought. What I really needed was a study savior.

As soon as I got home, I cleaned up my room for our study session. I figured since Blake was from the East Coast, she was probably well traveled and way more sophisticated than I was. Her room probably had photos of her with famous people and her awards and trophies from sports teams, not babyish things like my old Cabbage Patch dolls, my collectible Barbies, my LOL Dolls, and my Hatchimals. I shoved all my dolls and stuffed animals into my closet and left out my ribbons and awards of achievement and my photo with Nia and our dads at a Beyoncé concert last year. My room looked more . . . mature. Ready for Blake's arrival.

I quickly pulled on an oversized white T-shirt and a pair of jeans and slid the printed silk headband that Nia had bought for me this summer around my head. I finished off the look with a spritz of my Bath and Body Works vanilla sugar body spray.

The doorbell rang, and I bounded down the steps to open the door. Blake's hair looked like it had just been freshly straightened, and she had on a denim jacket and a black T-shirt and black jeans. Her mom stood beside her in almost the same outfit. They looked like sisters.

"Hello!" I said. "Come in, my mom is just making some snacks."

Blake breezed into our kitchen. She smelled like strawberries. I didn't know what perfume she wore, but it sure smelled expensive. My mother was standing at the kitchen island putting together hummus, pretzels, and some veggie sticks on a platter.

"Blake, it's nice to finally meet you. And hi, Ericka, how are you? My husband has told me a lot about you."

"It's great to be here," Blake's mom said warmly. "I'll be back for Blake before dinner. Is that all right?"

"Of course!" Mom answered. The women chatted as Mom walked Mrs. Williams to the door.

"Your house is really nice," Blake said.

"Thanks! We've been here as long as I can remember, I guess," I said.

"Did someone live here before you?"

I didn't know the answer to that. "Maybe? Maybe someone famous? Had to be, since this house is old," I said, trying to impress Blake. "Most old houses in Featherstone Creek were built by someone rich or famous." I thought so, anyway.

Suddenly, I got a horrible itch in my nose, an itch that I couldn't scratch or stop. It was one of Victoria's lie detector signals! I scrunched my face, trying desperately not to give in to the impending sneeze explosion.

Blake looked at me, confused. I had to come clean—this was torture! "Okay, really I don't know who lived here before us."

"It's okay, I don't know who lived in our house before, either," Blake said with a laugh. The itch immediately went away. *Gee, thanks, Victoria.*

I was eager to change the subject. "Where should we study?"

"Here's fine with me," Blake said. Guess I didn't need to rearrange my room after all. I could have spent that time studying instead, so I wouldn't look like such a math dunce in front of Blake.

We spread our books across the kitchen table, pushing the snacks to the far corner. Blake took out her notes. "Let me see your quiz."

I was hesitant to show her, primarily because I hadn't even told my parents yet that I had gotten a C minus. I didn't want either one of them to find out, and thankfully

they hadn't remembered to ask about it yet. And I *especially* didn't want them to find out in front of Blake—it would be the humiliation of my life! I carefully slid the quiz across the table, hiding the grade with my hand.

"I think you just need to go over the formulas a few more times when you study, and then you should be all set. Just dedicate one hour at a time to studying each chapter. That's how I do it. Poco a poco," Blake said breezily.

I didn't know what that meant. "Yeah, yes, of course."

Blake looked at me. "Do you know what that means?"

I froze. What I really wanted to do was play cool and pretend I knew, but in Victoria's eyes that was a lie. Immediately another crazy itch came on inside my nose. It was so strong, I felt my toes curling in my sneakers, and my hands shook from trying not to reach up and scratch it. One more second and I would sneeze all over Blake, the snacks, and our homework, and she would never want to be my friend again! I had to tell the truth. Curse you, Victoria! I blushed deeply and admitted in a small voice, "No."

Blake smiled back at me and the itch unfurled. "It means 'little by little' in Spanish. As in, you don't have to study and master everything at once. Just study a little at a time." Blake spoke Spanish, too? If my dad ever met Blake, he'd try to adopt her. I'd be sent off to an orphanage in a second.

We spent time reviewing the new information that

Mrs. Charles had gone over in today's class. For some reason, things seemed much clearer when Blake explained them to me. I didn't know if it was Blake's voice or the way she broke down each formula step-by-step, but I felt that I understood much better with her help. I digested the day's homework assignment easily.

We ate, we laughed, we even took a few selfies of us studying. Somehow, two hours flew by.

"I suppose my mom will be outside shortly. I should probably start packing up." Blake stacked her books inside of her book bag.

Mom reappeared in the kitchen. "Did you finish studying already?"

"Yes, ma'am," Blake said. "June's a whiz at math."

I didn't say anything—thank God that was Blake's lie and not mine! I mean, I *could* be a whiz at math if I kept studying. But right now, I didn't feel like anything about math was a whiz.

"Also, do you know that your daughter is one of the best field hockey players I've ever seen?" Blake said. "Her footwork is just so natural."

Mom started beaming, and I couldn't stop a big smile from stretching across my face in response. "Well, her father has wanted to put her in field hockey since she was about six. I guess he spotted her natural talent early on."

"I guess so. I think you've got the makings of a champion here," Blake said.

I could not believe how big Blake was talking me up. And if I couldn't believe it, surely my *mother* couldn't believe it either, right? Was Victoria listening? Could Blake feel that same annoying itchy-nose signal for lying *about* me? I peered around the room, looking for Victoria. No fairy dust anywhere. So others could lie about me, but I couldn't lie about myself. I mentally tucked that piece of the puzzle away for later—maybe it would help me figure out how to overcome the curse.

"I better go," Blake said. "My mom just texted me that she's outside."

"I'll walk you out," I said. My mom followed us.

Blake's mother sat in her red Mercedes parked in our driveway. As we walked to the car, she called out to my mom. "Hi! I hope Blake wasn't too much trouble."

"Oh, girl, please, Blake's nothing but an angel," my mom replied. "How's everything going? Are you settling in fine?"

"Oh yeah. Just getting used to the noise of construction at our place."

"I'll bet," my mom said. "Well, would you all want to come over for Sunday dinner, maybe this weekend? To escape the noise and construction at your place?"

My eyes lit up. *That would be awesome!*

"Let me confirm with my husband what he's got going on this week. I'll call you!"

"All right, great," my mom said with a smile. Guess

our parents were about to be friends, too. I eagerly waved to Blake, who had plopped herself in the front seat of the car.

"See you tomorrow in class," Blake said. The Mercedes pulled off and we waved from the driveway. My mother walked toward the house, but I waited a beat, watching Blake's car get smaller as it drove down the street. I smiled. Even though I didn't know Spanish, wasn't good at math, and had to fight back a sneeze attack while sitting a few feet from her face, she still wanted to come back and hang out. Is it possible the truth didn't have to ruin my *entire* life?

CONFESSION #6:

Victoria is everywhere. Listening to every single conversation I have! Like today, when Blake came over, and I couldn't even tell a little white lie about understanding Blake's Spanish without getting a lie detector signal from her. I was just trying to impress a new friend! I really like her. But I can't sneak anything past that Victoria. Why can't I figure out how to get around this spell already? I can solve a Rubik's Cube, I always finish Grandma's sudoku puzzles! Blake's coming for Sunday dinner soon, so I don't have much time to figure out how to get around my weird truth-telling issue. I'm lucky all that sneezing and me admitting the truth about not knowing even the most basic Spanish didn't drive away someone I was trying to impress.

CHAPTER TEN

✦ ✦
✦

Nia texted me on Friday afternoon.

> **NIA:** Remember me?

> **JUNE:** I see you in class every day!

> **NIA:** I know but we can't have real talk in class.

Between field hockey, the school paper, and homework, I hadn't spent much time with anyone after school lately, let alone made any time for myself. I was exhausted, and so overwhelmed by all the responsibilities and pressure swirling around me. After I came home from practice on Friday I fell straight into bed—I didn't even have the energy to take my backpack or my shoes off. Thank goodness for cell phones. If we couldn't text, we'd never talk at all, even about the important things. Like whether Nia should get bangs.

NIA: Can we make an actual date to hang?

JUNE: When?

NIA: This weekend? Have you seen Olive?

JUNE: No. We've been texting about English stuff, but I haven't seen her either.

I'm free Sunday.

NIA: Okay, Sunday. After church. I'll
tell Olive, too.

JUNE: Cool.

Wait. Oh no. I forgot we had plans. On Sunday Blake's
family would be coming over for dinner. I was really looking forward to it.

JUNE: Oh wait. Can't on Sunday.
Family stuff.

That was true. Sort of. But maybe not. Dang it! If it was technically the truth, could I still get in trouble with Victoria? I didn't need her to show up or see our texts!

I pulled up the home screen for my secret blog on my phone and typed in a quick entry:

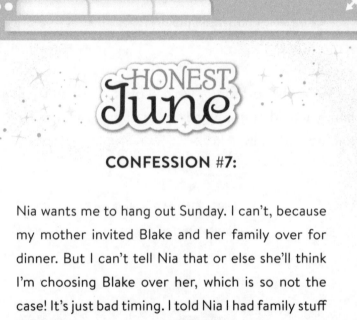

CONFESSION #7:

Nia wants me to hang out Sunday. I can't, because my mother invited Blake and her family over for dinner. But I can't tell Nia that or else she'll think I'm choosing Blake over her, which is so not the case! It's just bad timing. I told Nia I had family stuff so she wouldn't get jealous and explode on me. It wasn't technically a lie—but it wasn't really the truth, either. This sort of drama is bad for my skin.

Wait a minute. Could I get around the curse by answering questions with another truth, even if it wasn't the *real* real truth? Like, if someone asked me if my favorite color is pink and I told them that my favorite color *isn't* purple but didn't outright lie and say it's pink?! I looked around the room. No dust. No Victoria. I was safe. For the moment. And I may have just discovered a workaround. . . . For a brief second I was flying high about my discovery, until—

Nia texted back. **Family stuff? Like what?**

Oh nooo, Nia, don't go there! I said to myself. I tried to ignore the text. But Nia wouldn't let up—she grilled me. **Hello! What family stuff?**

I needed to lie. There was *no way* I could tell Nia the truth. She'd be really mad—like, lose-my-number mad. She would never speak to me again. I would lose her friendship and then Olive's, and then Blake wouldn't want to hang out with me, and then I would become a social outcast at school, and no one would talk to me for the rest of my life, and I would *die alone*! I started to feel a tingling in my hands, and my nose twitched. Victoria was sending a lie detector signal. The itching got stronger, and I sneezed once. Then again. The sneezes got louder and more powerful, my whole body racked with sneezes, and the feeling in my chest started building and building, and the only thing I could do to stop it was to tell the truth! Hands shaking, I responded to Nia's text: **My mom invited the Williamses over for dinner.**

A minute passed before she responded. **As in Blake Williams's family?**

> **JUNE: Yes, Nia.**

> **NIA: Oh, I see how it is.**

I sucked my teeth. My fingers moved faster than my mind as I typed a response.

> **JUNE: You see how what is? My mother invited them over during our study session.**

> **NIA: You studied together?**

> **JUNE: Yeah?**

Nia waited another minute before typing her response. **Aiight, girl. Whatever. Replace me with Blake, it's cool.**

Was Nia being her usual dramatic self or was I actually dumping my bestie-since-birth friendship straight into the toilet?

I'm not replacing you! Can we meet after school on Monday? I'm free, I swear, I responded. I was off from the school paper then. Ms. West was out for the day and had canceled our weekly pitch session. Which meant I had the afternoon free to hang with Nia and Olive, no excuses. I had to do this. If I didn't make time to see them this week, I could count on being alone for the rest of my life for sure.

Monday, Nia replied, mercifully. **I'll tell Olive. Ice cream at Dips. Don't be late. And did you find my bracelet yet? Don't try to keep it for yourself!** What she didn't say, although I knew she was thinking it, was that this was my last chance to salvage my closest friendships before they were gone for good. I ignored the inquiry about the bracelet, looked around for any sign of Victoria, tossed my phone beside me on the bed, and let out a big, mind-clearing sigh.

✦

My mother did not invite people over to our house to be polite—those invitations were rare. If she invited you over for Sunday dinner, you were coming to Sunday dinner to be welcomed as part of the family or, at the very least, as new friends. I put on my Sunday best—the fancy blouse

I'd bought from Fit, with a camisole underneath, and a denim skirt.

I gave myself some extra time to shower, do my hair, and put on a bit of lip gloss. I had downloaded a few songs Blake suggested I listen to on a Spotify playlist she shared with me after practice the other day—mostly remixes of Ariana Grande and Beyoncé songs.

Blake and her parents were expected around 4:30 p.m., so I came downstairs right after 4:00. Mom was in the kitchen, seasoning a pot of sautéed collard greens. (Great—another opportunity for a Victoria-sponsored sneeze attack. Was I finally going to have to admit I hated them?)

"June, darling, are you really wearing that to dinner?" she said.

Uh-oh. "Yeah," I answered. "I like it." I held my breath.

"Yes, honey, but I don't. Why don't you put on that Mickey Mouse shirt I picked out for you? Then you can throw your jacket over your shoulders if you get cold." Mom had bought the shirt when we went to Disney World two years ago, and it was two sizes too big then. It fit better now, but it had the words "when you wish upon a star" scrawled in pink cursive letters. And it wasn't just Mickey on the shirt. All the chipmunks, ducks, and dog characters were arranged in a circle around him. *Why not put the training wheels back on my bike while you're at it, Mom?* I couldn't wear this shirt in front of Blake. She was so cool and stylish—it would be humiliating. Uh-oh . . .

"Because I—" I started. Feelings bubbled up in my throat, but I stopped myself from getting the words out. I didn't want to start a fight with my mom this close to dinner with Blake. My nose began to itch.

"You can't what? Mickey goes better with the skirt anyway. And it gets a bit chilly at night, so you need to be more covered up than that shirt."

I looked back at her with flat eyes. I desperately wanted to tell her to take that Mickey Mouse shirt and burn it on the barbecue. The word vomit rose in my chest. Then to my throat. I had to sneeze! Or actually vomit?! I had to run away before I exploded.

As I ran up the stairs, the word vomit was ready to spew. I dashed into my room, just before I felt my mouth open. I shut the door and exhaled.

"June, honey?" My mom knocked on the door. "Everything all right?"

My mouth was ready to spit fire. I didn't know whether I was going to spew words or *actual* vomit. I had never felt so sick to my stomach! Where was my computer? I grabbed it, opened up the screen, and pulled up the blog. I typed fast:

HONEST June

CONFESSION #8:

I want to wear my Fit shirt, not Mickey and his band of animals from the Magic Kingdom! Because that Mickey shirt makes me look like a baby, and the shirt from Fit I picked out makes me look like a young woman!

I collapsed on the bed. I had gotten out the truth before anyone could hear me. I realized I'd been tensing my shoulders and my stomach and tried to relax them, but my body fought with me. I felt like I'd been hit by a truck.

"Mmmmmmm," I mumbled. I had felt better as I typed, as if the word vomit was coming through my fingertips instead of my mouth. The pressure began decreasing in my stomach and my head, but I still felt like my insides were swirling.

"Are you changing clothes? Your friend will be here shortly." When was this going to end?!

I typed into the computer:

> I don't want to change clothes! Mom, when are you going to realize I am not a child anymore?!

Then I sat back and tried to keep my breathing steady. I looked at my closet. I knew I'd have to put on the Mickey Mouse shirt so she'd be happy and dinner could go smoothly and we would look like the perfect family in front of the Williamses. Putting on Mickey meant peace in our house, even if I would be humiliating myself in front of my new potential friend. Blake would never want to hang out with me after this. "Yes, Mom," I said, and I was surprised to hear that I sounded like I was nearly on the verge of tears.

"Good. I'll see you downstairs."

I heard her footsteps fade away toward the staircase. I looked toward my closet, and typed one last sentence in the blog:

> I will change. I resent it, but I'm doing this just so I don't have a fight at the dinner table.
>
> ✦

I pulled off the Fit shirt, hung it back up in the closet, and slipped on the Mickey Mouse shirt. As I rolled up the sleeves and slid on a stack of big bangles, I contemplated this latest symptom. I'd honestly felt like I was going to vomit—I'd never felt so nauseated before in my life! Was this a new bit of fun courtesy of Victoria? Or was I actually sick? I tried to shake off the feeling of tension, and headed back downstairs just as the doorbell rang.

✦

I heard hands slapping as my dad greeted Mr. Williams when he walked in, and the clickety-clack of high heels as my mom and Blake's mom walked through the house toward the backyard. With her mom and dad by her side, I noticed that Blake had her mother's eyes and smile but her dad's deep brown skin tone and basketball-player height.

Blake wore a red dress that came to her knees and black flats that looked expensive. In fact, they looked like shoes her mother might wear. Why couldn't I be that classy and cool? I felt another wave of nausea when I remembered what I was wearing. Blake smiled wide when she saw me. "Hey, girl!"

"Hey," I said, hiding behind a chair in the kitchen so Blake wouldn't see my shirt. "Did you just come from church?"

"You're funny. That was hours ago," Blake replied.

We made our way through the backyard, and I did my best to walk behind Blake so she wouldn't see my outfit. Throughout dinner, my dad and Mr. Williams chatted about sports and politics and a few recent cases about famous people that the local paper had reported on. The moms talked about their houses and various friends they both knew. Blake and I sat together at the end of the table, leaning in to talk about things we didn't want the parents to hear.

"How's math going?" she asked.

"Still crappy," I said. That was the truth.

"Well, we have another quiz next week. You have plenty of time to study."

In between bites of sweet potatoes, my mom began to pepper Blake with questions, and she politely answered each one. "Yes, Dr. Jackson," "No, Dr. Jackson," "I might, Dr. Jackson."

Then Mr. Williams casually launched a ton of bricks at me and asked the question that I dreaded anyone asking. Particularly now, while under a truth-telling spell by a fairy godmother: "So, do you want to be a lawyer like your father, June?"

I froze. I looked at Mr. Williams with wide eyes, like I'd just seen a ghost. I couldn't answer this. I didn't want to. The itching in my nose immediately began, and I swore I saw a glimmer of fairy dust out of the corner of my eye. I caught my tongue between my teeth and crossed my fingers, brain moving a mile a second, desperately trying to calculate how to get myself out of this one. The silence lingered for what seemed like minutes until my father spoke up for me. "Of course she does! We've already put our HU JD 2035 strategy in place!" he said, toasting and sipping his glass of wine.

I pursed my lips together even tighter. *Hold it in, June, just hold it in.* My dad spoke up again, turning to Blake. "And, Blake, do you want to follow in your father's footsteps?"

Had these two dads decided it was "Put Our Daughters on Blast" night? I turned quickly to Blake, hoping to God her response would distract the table from my discomfort. Luckily, Blake handled her time in the hot seat much better.

"Absolutely," Blake said with conviction.

My mouth relaxed. My moment had passed. Blake's dad beamed in his chair, proud of his little girl. My dad's face lit up at hearing Blake's answer, his eyebrows rising high on his forehead. "All right! Another lawyer in the family! See, our little girls will take over the firm when we're ready to retire," he said.

I sank further in my chair, bit my tongue, and prayed this dinner would end quickly without any more cross-examination.

HONEST June

CONFESSION #9:

That was one of the most difficult Sunday dinners I've ever had to endure. One, because I was trying so hard to be cool in front of Blake, and I had to keep contorting my body behind plates and trays and the table so she wouldn't see my shirt and judge me. And, two, because I failed to answer Mr. Williams's questions about my future plans in front of my parents, and I could tell it disappointed them. I know Dad wants me to be a lawyer. I know that would help continue the family business and grow our legacy. But honestly, I don't want to be a lawyer. I don't even think I want to go to Howard. And the worst part of all is the hard truth: that I'm only 11 years old, and I have no idea what I want to be when I grow up. But how do I explain that to my parents without looking like a failure in their eyes?

Monday morning began with work and more work. Mrs. Charles assigned two chapters' worth of math homework for the night. Plus, my geology report was due Tuesday morning for science class. As I went to each classroom, a headache throbbed harder across my temples. It seemed like more and more homework was being assigned, as if each teacher knew I would have an extra few hours after school and was trying to grab dibs on them. Each time I walked out of a classroom, sweat had dampened either my upper lip or my armpits.

At lunch, Nia and Olive chatted intensely as they sat down across from me. "Hey, y'all," I said. They barely heard me and continued to talk.

"Hello? Remember me?" I said with a wave.

"Girl, we see you," Nia said, and rolled her eyes. "You good?"

"Yeah, you?"

"Peachy keen," Olive said.

"Peachy keen?" I said. I'd never heard her use that phrase. I raised one eyebrow.

Olive looked at Nia and they laughed. "Oh yeah, just a little inside joke from this weekend."

"You hung out this weekend?" My chest felt heavy knowing they hung out without me. It wasn't the first time, but now, when Nia and I were in a weird place and I was under this spell that exposed my true feelings to the world, I felt especially vulnerable. Was this the beginning of the end of our friendships?

"Yeah," Nia continued. "Since you were . . . busy." That tone was typical of unmistakably annoyed Nia.

At the end of lunch, just before I went to my next class, I got an email on my tablet from Ms. West. Even though she'd been out for the school day, she was calling an all-hands meeting after school for a special presentation. By whom or about what she didn't say—just that we all had to be there. My heart sank. I'd have to cancel my meetup with Nia and Olive—the one we'd planned before the weekend. The one I was desperately looking forward to. I shoveled chicken noodle soup into my mouth, brainstorming how to break the news.

Nia spoke up, interrupting my concentration on my email and its consequences. "Don't eat too much. Remember, we're going to Dips after school."

I looked away from Nia. I dreaded her reaction to my schedule conflict. "Um, I can't go anymore," I said quietly. "I have a newspaper meeting thing."

"A newspaper meeting? I thought you said those were on Wednesdays."

"The mandatory meetings are Wednesdays. Mondays are usually optional, for pitching story ideas and stuff.

But today's a special meeting, and everyone's required to show up," I explained.

Nia sat back in her chair and crossed her arms. "Dang, girl. Well, Olive, you still down?"

"Yes, indeed. I'm craving mint chip."

"Is there no orchestra today?" I asked. They were going to hang out without me *again*?

"Practice on Mondays is optional," Olive explained. "We usually practice at home, then bring whatever questions we have about the pieces to rehearsal Tuesday."

Nia turned her head and focused on Olive. "So, I'll meet you at the entrance at three?"

"Yup," Olive answered.

I felt like an outsider. I went back to sipping my chicken noodle soup while Nia and Olive planned the rest of their afternoon without me. I hated missing good times with my friends. Particularly if it involved ice cream. And especially if it seemed like the demise of our good times was approaching.

✦

After school, I saw Nia and Olive meet each other at the entrance and head off to Dips together. I headed toward the newspaper office, wishing I could eat ice cream with my friends and erase the tension to fix everything between us instead.

Turns out, Ms. West had brought in a special guest writer, Leticia Simmons, a graduate of Featherstone Creek Middle School who was now a famous author and journalist. She talked about the responsibilities of being a reporter and telling stories that had the power to help people. As I listened, I could have sworn I saw Victoria's eyes flash in Leticia's as she said the word *truth* over and over again. "Journalism is about telling the truth no matter who it benefits, because in the end your story should always benefit the reader," she said. She made a good point about truth being beneficial. Maybe this is what Victoria was trying to get me to understand all along? I mean, sure, I could acknowledge that telling the truth about, like, famines and wars and corruption could benefit human-kind. But I still wasn't exactly seeing how my little white lies to keep my family and friends happy weren't beneficial to all of us in the end.

Leticia's lecture was only about twenty-five minutes, so I had plenty of time to walk home or even catch up with the girls at Dips. I rushed out of the room, hustling to zip up my backpack as I ran, hoping to catch my friends. I had just stepped out of the school's front entrance when I spotted Lee at the back end of the main hallway, perhaps waiting for one of his grandparents to pick him up. I called out to him, and he ran up to me.

"Hey," he said, "what are you still doing here?"

"I had a school newspaper meeting," I said.

"Ah, cool. We had a Creeks meeting." *Oh, the Creeks!* It felt like a million years since Lee and I had hung out and he encouraged me to join the club.

"I keep wanting to go, but I can't find the time," I said sadly.

"It's okay, you'll catch the next one. You headed out?" he asked.

"Yeah, you walking?"

"Yeah. C'mon," he said, and gestured me forward.

We stepped out the main doors, and my face felt warmer as the late-afternoon sun beamed down on me. I did miss Lee's company, a lot. Normally, we got to meet up at least once a week, usually Sunday mornings

right after church. But I hadn't had time to ride my bike through the neighborhood with him. I hadn't even met his pet lizard, Chadwick, yet. And worst of all, I'd been so busy worrying about everything else that I hadn't realized I was being a bad friend to Lee, too.

"So, what's cracking?" he asked me. I looked at Lee's face, immediately guilty. I don't know if it was my feelings of missing him or my guilt over forgetting that we were even good friends, but I couldn't help spilling my guts.

"Me!" I began. "I knew sixth grade would be busy, but not this nuts! I can't seem to keep up with classes, homework, field hockey, the school paper. . . . And I've barely had time for my friends. I haven't seen you outside of school since before school started! I need like four more hours in the day. And even then, I'm not sure if it would be enough time to do all the stuff I have to do."

"Yeah, me too," Lee said. "Mrs. Charles is no joke when it comes to that math homework!"

"No doubt," I said. That was the truth. "I mean, she must be grading on a curve, right?"

"I dunno. I was talking to Alvin about it, and he heard she never rounds up or grades on a curve. If you flunk, you flunk—that's her motto."

Oh my gosh, I couldn't end up with a C in her class. If I got a C, it would be the beginning of failure for the rest of my life! "I hate math," I blurted out. The everlasting truth. Here it comes. I was powerless to stop it. My heart started racing. "I can't ever memorize the equations. I feel so stupid. I even tried writing the equations in the notes file of my tablet, but then I felt guilty about cheating." I slapped my hand over my mouth.

Why did I just admit that to him? Why, oh why can't I stop talking?! "Oh man, I can't believe I just said that," I said.

"Dude, everyone I know hates math," Lee said. "And everyone I know has tried the same thing. Don't sweat it. Just remember, the school tablets save what you type into the notes app, so watch yourself."

We'd walked off the campus down Main Street to Houston Street, the one that winds in front of my house, then continued on to connect with the street that Lee lives on. On the corner, right across the street from us, was Dips. I realized this only at the exact moment Nia and Olive walked up to us, just as I was word vomiting my dislike for math class to Lee—to my horror.

"Hey, girl," Nia said, clearly frustrated. "You too busy for us, but not too busy for him?" Her tone was not pleasant.

Lee could sense the tension. He defended me. "We just ran into each other in the hallway."

Nia rocked back on one hip and crossed her arms. "But we made plans. We then changed those plans because you had family stuff, and then today you had the paper. But now here you are, with him."

A thick silence overtook us. Olive also looked surprised and disappointed. "Dang, girl, really?" she added.

"No!" I finally said loudly, after gaping at my friends for a good chunk of time. I didn't want to offend Lee, but I had to make my point. "I had just left my paper meeting. I was on my way home, and Lee saw me in the hallway, and we were chatting about math class, and here we are. I swear!"

"Uh-huh," Nia said.

"Nia, you *know* I'm not lying!" I begged her.

Lee looked at the girls with a puzzled look on his face, clearly uncomfortable. "June, I can catch up with you later," he said, backing away and walking toward his house.

"No, Lee, wait," I said, and turned to catch him before he left.

"So, you do have time to hang out, or you don't?" Nia said.

"No! I mean, yes. I mean, I didn't, but now I do," I said. I had even confused myself.

"C'mon, Olive, June's busy," Nia said. She turned on her heel before I could say anything else, truth or lie. Olive pursed her lips and looked toward the ground and followed Nia.

"I didn't mean . . ." I tried to get some kind of explanation out of my mouth. But it was too late. The girls had walked off, leaving me on the sidewalk alone. Lee was already halfway down the block heading home. I was honest about getting out of the meeting early and unexpectedly running into Lee, but the truth still didn't help me. The truth was never going to set me free. And as I turned back toward my house, I wondered if any of my friends would ever talk to me again.

HONEST June

CONFESSION #10:

What in the world just happened? I had a last-minute newspaper meeting that ended early, I happened to see Lee, and we happened to walk home together. It was all very innocent, but Nia thought I planned to ditch her all along! Believe me, I'm desperate to hang out with Nia and Olive. They're my best friends and I've barely had time to talk to them even via text because I'm so busy running around between school and field hockey and the paper. I wish I could find more time in the day to do all the things I want to do.

Why can't Victoria create a way to make time stand still so I can do everything I want and never miss out on anything? I'd rather have THAT superpower than this annoying truth-telling one! I'm just not believing that it's doing any good, and I don't believe it's helping. Telling the truth is the hardest thing I've ever done, and I don't see that changing anytime soon. And it seems like I'm further away than ever from proving to Victoria that it's easier for me to tell the truth than lie.

CHAPTER ELEVEN

✦✦✦

We usually ate dinner together as a family by 6:00 p.m. if Dad didn't have to prepare for a trial or Mom didn't have to deliver any babies. Sometimes it was a quick dinner, with Dad shoveling food in his face as fast as possible so he could get back to work. But the days where he had time, he took that time to put *me* on trial. And tonight, Monday night, during a dinner of sweet and spicy chicken wings and salad, court was in session.

"What's going on at school, baby girl? How you doing in your classes?" he asked.

"I'm hanging in there," I answered after a pause. For now, that was the truth. Between field hockey, paper, school, and friend drama, I *was* just barely hanging on.

Dad took a bite of chicken. "There's a debate team at

school, right? You should join. It's a great start for your career as a lawyer."

I looked at him in horror. This debate thing again! For one, I wasn't interested. As far as I knew, it was a club for people to fight over things, and I couldn't take any more of that kind of drama. It was enough trying to concentrate on not failing math or tripping over my own two feet on the field hockey pitch when I had a fairy godmother watching over me and two friends mad at me. And between classes and all my extracurriculars and responsibilities, how could I possibly have time for another activity? I was struggling to find the time to finish my homework as is! Did my Dad really think I wasn't doing enough?!

Oh, and let's not forget that dreaded C minus in math that I still hadn't told my parents about!

That nervous bubbling crept up in my stomach again and I leaned away from my plate, the sight of food suddenly making my insides churn. *Maybe if I just laugh it off, he'll forget about this.* "Ha! Dad."

"What's funny?" he asked with a furrowed brow.

Not the reaction I expected. Dang. I started to feel hot, and my temples began to pound. "Nothing, I just . . ." I started panicking. The itch in my nose was back. Victoria was pushing me to tell the truth to my Dad about how overwhelmed I was—I could feel it. My fingers twitched for my phone, but I realized it was in my bag upstairs, so I couldn't type a quick entry into my blog to get around telling the truth. I whipped my head around the room, looking for an out.

"June?" Dad said. "Really, is something wrong?" Mom looked up from her plate. The uncomfortable feeling rushed from my stomach and through my throat, where it settled into a big ball in my chest. My mouth became dry, like it was full of cotton balls. I couldn't escape this. As my dad licked clean his third chicken wing, a rush of word vomit that I knew was going to kick off a very uncomfortable conversation spewed from my mouth.

"I can barely fit in an hour each week to see my best friends on top of schoolwork and field hockey *and* the school paper! Plus, I have *zero* interest in the debate club. Zero! Maybe standing around arguing with a bunch of brainiacs is your idea of a good time, but it's not mine! I'm on the field hockey team already because you wanted me to be. Isn't that enough?"

Dad glared; it felt like his gaze went right into my skull. He leaned back in his seat and wiped his mouth with the cloth napkin. I knew I had said too much, and I knew the next words out of his mouth were going to burn my feelings into charred toast.

"Since you have some strong opinions on what you do and do not have time for, I'm going to give you my strong words of advice. You *will* make the time and try out for the debate team. I was on the debate team when I was a kid. As well as the football team. I had enough time to be athletic *and* smart. And I went on to found my own law firm."

I felt unexpected tears begin to prick my eyes. Mom interjected, "Honey, go easy on her. If she's not interested, she's not interested."

I rocked back and forth, hoping nothing else would come out of my mouth that could further offend my dad. Why did I leave my phone upstairs this one time? Every other dinner, I snuck it under the table just in case Nia texted, and this *one time* I left it upstairs—because I knew she wouldn't text me, because she wasn't speaking to me now.

Dad leaned forward again. "If you want to be a lawyer, you're going to have to learn to debate. Or at least express your feelings with logic, not just uncontrollable emotions"—he stood up, emphasizing his words even further—"so you don't take that tone with me again."

I felt like a cold blast of air had frozen me in place in my chair. I was *mortified*. Not only had I defied my dad, but I had insulted him, too. Could I be any worse as a daughter? I might as well have said he'd wasted his entire life becoming a lawyer! All this just because I felt scared to put one more activity on my plate. And because I was honest about my not wanting to pursue debate! This is what Victoria's honesty got me—my family's scorn and disappointment!

I blinked, faster and faster, hoping I could make myself disappear if I just blinked fast enough. Dad walked toward the kitchen. Maybe to get away from me, the disrespectful daughter who was destined to be a failure because she wouldn't have a strong enough debate background to be a lawyer. Or maybe he just wanted another chicken wing from the platter on the counter. I didn't know. What I did know was that I had made my dad super angry and super disappointed, which was the last thing I wanted to do. I had never full-on gone against my parents' wishes before, even when I didn't want to do what they wanted. I was too scared of the consequences, and I knew I had a good thing going at home. By obeying my parents, I earned their respect, I was rewarded with nice things, I even earned my own Netflix user profile to watch what I wanted! But now that all seemed to be in jeopardy. Man, the truth freaking hurts.

◆

After dinner, I went upstairs to my room. Not because I was on punishment. Or was I? I might as well have been, after how my dad spoke to me. His reaction to me telling the truth was worse than if I had kept my feelings to myself and actually joined the debate club and started picking fights with random people (or whatever they do).

I felt burnt. If I did debate, I'd completely burn out from trying to fit in one more activity. And I'd be toast by not doing debate and telling my parents how I really felt. This was what the truth did to people? This was supposed to help me live a better life? What was Victoria thinking?

Just then, I coughed. The air seemed to have gotten rather thick. Then a gray film started to form, a cloud, a poof of recognizable dust. *Here she comes. Victoria.* She floated into my room gently, then flopped onto the floor as if she'd missed her landing mark, knocking her tiara to the side of her head.

"Drat, I really have to get better at the landings," she said. "Hello, dear. How are you?"

I looked at her, my head drooping to one side. "Uh, doing horribly?"

"What's the matter? What, that thing with your dad?"

"Yeah, and the thing with Nia, and the other thing. This truth-telling thing is making my life miserable!"

"You've told the truth, and now you don't have to lie to your dad about debate," she countered, arms high to the sky. "Win! Win!"

"I told the truth and now he hates me! If I don't get out of this curse, I'm going to have no friends *and* no dad! What can I do? Money? Can I pay you? Valuables? What do you want? Look around! You can have anything! Just get me out of this spell!" She had no idea what my life was like—how many people I had to please and keep from getting hurt! If I had lied at the dinner table and said I'd consider doing debate, I could've avoided all the drama, the disappointment. Lying was *way* easier than upsetting Dad with the truth.

"You're hilarious! Honey, I don't need money. I pay for everything in fairy dust. Now, June, living a life of lies will not help you keep relationships and get ahead in life," Victoria said. "Trust me. The truth is not always easy, but it is the key to a good life."

"I don't believe you."

"Well, telling the truth is the only way I'll lift the spell. Remember, the only opinion that matters is your own. People may not like what you say, or they may not want to hear what you truly believe, but they can't stay mad at you forever for telling the truth. Trust me."

Before I could argue any more with her, she stood upright and started turning in quick circles. Fairy dust swirled around her, creating a funnel that then swooped her away into thin air. While the remnants of her magic sprinkles and debris settled, I felt like I could hear my heartbeat pounding in my ears. I flopped onto my bed, trying to find a minute of relief. But instead of slowing down, my heart started beating faster. It felt like a rocket was trying to take off inside my chest. I shook my head. *No, I'm just imagining things.* Then my palms grew sweaty. The room seemed smaller than usual. I felt like the walls were moving toward me. I breathed more heavily, and it was harder for me to get each breath in and out. *Oh gosh, what's happening?* Why was I panicking? Tears started leaking from my eyes. I just need a break. . . .

I just, *I just*—

I grabbed for my phone and texted Chloe. **911.**

A few seconds later, my phone rang. "What's wrong? June? What happened?" Chloe said frantically.

"I got into a fight with my dad," I said, the tears falling freely.

"How in the world did you do that?" she asked.

"I told him the truth about what I thought about the debate team." I held back a sob.

"Why were you talking about the debate team?"

"He wants me to join. I said I didn't have time," I blubbered.

"Oof! Might as well tell him you hate Howard."

I shook my head and my voice rose a few octaves. "I'm just too busy to take on debate!"

"Did you tell him that?"

"Of course, Chloe," I cried. "But he wasn't having it!"

"He'll get there, June. The only way you're going to get anything done when it comes to your parents is if you tell them the truth."

"But I can't talk to them! If I tell them the truth, they'll be disappointed, and I can't lie to them because I literally *cannot lie*!"

"Calm down," Chloe urged. "Take a few deep breaths. Don't hyperventilate on me."

I opened the window. The air was crisp and helped me clear my mind of my racing thoughts. I took a few deep breaths until my face returned to a normal temperature and my eyes dried. My palms felt less sweaty. I felt myself calming down.

The truth had not set me free. It had done nothing but make me a prisoner of my own thoughts.

I took another big breath and let my shoulders relax. My heart slowed down a few beats. Chloe was still on the line. "You need to talk to someone who will help you find a way to manage all your responsibilities. Is there anyone you can trust?"

There was one and only one person who came to mind.

CHAPTER TWELVE

On my way to a meeting for the school newspaper on Wednesday, I stopped into the library to find a book Mr. Brown had assigned for social studies class. I glanced at the school bulletin board and saw the same black-and-white debate team flyer I'd spotted earlier. I could see my dad's face in front of me, his voice bellowing in my head. "You will join the debate team. You will be a lawyer. You will go to Howard." Like he was a ventriloquist. And I was the dummy.

I read the flyer out loud, thinking I could hypnotize myself into being interested in joining debate. IF YOU'RE PASSIONATE & HAVE BIG IDEAS, YOU'LL FIND YOUR PLACE HERE, it said. I'm certainly passionate. And I could have big ideas, too. Maybe I should just go to one meeting after all. . . .

My stomach started to bubble, and the feeling of

nausea appeared. I reached my hand forward to rip off one of the dangly pieces of paper with the words "Debate Team" and an email address to contact. As my hand moved toward the paper, my stomach flip-flopped.

My dad wanted me to join. But *I* didn't want to. That was the truth—my stomach was telling me as much. I wrapped my arms around my middle, trying to keep my guts from churning.

All of a sudden, I saw fairy dust flicker in the corner of my eye. It got thicker and thicker in front of me, swirling until a form of a woman appeared. Long curly hair, broad smile. Tiara slightly crooked atop her head. My fairy godmother.

"Hello, dear," Victoria said, slightly out of breath and stumbling into view. "You are moving so fast these days, it's so hard to keep up with you!"

"Victoria!" I said. I glanced around the room to see if anyone else could see me talking to what they would think was thin air, since no one else could see Victoria. "You can't just pop up at my school! Security is tight here! At least I thought it is. . . ."

"Darling, I see you're debating joining the debate team," she said, "but I don't know why. You've already confessed to your dad that you don't want to do it."

"I don't," I said emphatically.

"Then why are you stressing yourself out about doing something you don't want to do?"

I started to back away from the flyer. "Because I thought . . . maybe I could find a way to force myself."

Victoria leaned over me and fairy dust fell on my shoulders. "And what good does that do? Except make you more miserable?"

"Yeah . . . ," I admitted.

"That's not a great feeling, June. Instead of following others' wishes, you have to follow your heart. Or in this case, your gut. Go with your gut, dear."

The farther I stepped away from the board and the debate club poster, the better my stomach felt. Victoria waved her wand over my head, creating a cloud of dust and sprinkles, and vanished into the swirl of glitter.

I knew she was right, but Dad was going to be so disappointed. I was totally going to get the eyebrows when he found out I'd made up my mind.

I turned out of the library, vowing to come back later for the social studies book, and headed to the newspaper office.

✦

My face looked like a grumpy cat's during the newspaper meeting. Ms. West must have picked up on my sad mood, because she called out, "June—want to come over here for a minute? Let's talk about some story ideas."

We sat in a corner of the office. I looked around

nervously. "So, what's going on, June?" Ms. West asked. "You don't seem like your usual chipper self."

"I *am* chipper," I said brightly, and instantly sneezed. It was a lie. My stomach swirled with anxiety. *Dang it, Victoria!* I'd just have to let this one go. I quickly came clean. "Okay, so maybe I'm not so chipper."

"I see," Ms. West said. "Is something going on? Something up with school?"

I took a deep breath as I fidgeted in my seat, deciding how best to answer. I felt the words rush up toward my mouth. I knew Victoria was listening, and I didn't want to have another sneeze attack. Plus, Ms. West was so cool. My defenses fell down almost instantly. "Okay, I'm miserable."

"What are you talking about?"

The words spilled out of me like a freight train rushing over a bridge. "My dad expects straight As, and for me to play field hockey and join the debate team. But I got a C minus on my math quiz, so he's going to freak out about that. And I'm also behind in social studies. And I only started playing field hockey because Dad wanted me to, but then I met this cool girl, Blake, so I'm really only on the team 'cause I can hang out with her. And then my dad wants me to join the debate team, and I just, I—I just can't do it all!"

I realized my voice had gotten louder and louder as I admitted the truth. I took a breath and assessed. This was what Victoria wanted me to do, right? Releasing the truth left me feeling light-headed. Light-headed, dizzy, and totally out of breath. I was not feeling like my regular self—that much was definitely true. Ms. West looked concerned. "Well, this is a lot, June. But it's good you're getting this all out."

I looked up at her. The light-headedness faded slightly. "I guess."

"Sounds like you have a lot on your plate," Ms. West said. "Let's start with what feels good. What do you have in your schedule that you genuinely enjoy doing, just for you?"

I looked at Ms. West. "I like writing," I said. "I've really enjoyed working on the paper so far. But I feel like my dad doesn't support any of the creative stuff. Only the 'get into Howard University' stuff."

I became very calm as I admitted all of this to Ms. West. Like something in me had finally unleashed.

She clasped her hands in front of her and leaned in close to me. "I feel you," Ms. West said. "Parents only want the best for their children. But, you know, it sounds like you're feeling pressure over trying to please everyone else instead of yourself. Maybe you should be honest with your parents about your feelings."

Funny you should mention that, Ms. West, I thought. "I don't think they would understand," I said.

"You won't know until you sit down to talk, but I think you should do that," she said. "I'm sure they'll understand if you explain your side of the situation."

"I don't know about that," I said, hesitant.

"Think about it, June." She leaned back in her chair and paused. "Do you want to take a break from the paper for a while until your grades come back up?"

"No!" I said. "The paper makes me happy. I just don't want my dad to hate me."

"Oh, well, it sounds like we'll need to help you find a balance between the time you spend studying and the time you spend on your extracurriculars," Ms. West said. "Do you want to review your schedule together and see where we can find some wiggle room? That includes the paper—maybe you should only commit to coming every other week? Will that help? You don't have to answer right away—think about it and decide what will work for you."

I scrunched my face in thought, and, with a smile, Ms. West got up and left me there to think. I stood up and walked out of the meeting room, headed to the bathroom, thinking a splash of cold water would help me settle down and plot a helpful next step. The hallway was quiet. I heard only the echo of my shoes on the floor as I walked.

I pushed open the door to the girls' bathroom. It was so silent in there, I could hear my heart beating. My mind drifted to the thought of telling my dad about my math grade and about not doing the debate team. I felt my breathing getting faster. The walls moved closer and closer toward me, like they had in my bedroom the other day. I went into one of the stalls and tried to use the restroom, but I felt so nervous and uptight that I couldn't even pee.

Suddenly I heard the door open. "Hello?" I called out. No one answered. I gathered my things and opened the stall door. Near the exit was a cleaning stand with mops and trash bags, and a woman with gray hair and a striped uniform hunched over the cart. "Oh, sorry, I didn't realize anyone was here," I said.

The woman turned around. I was expecting an older woman, but instead, the woman had a younger face. She was pretty, with a recognizable toothy grin and wide eyes. *Victoria.*

"Hello, darling!" she said in her usual chipper voice. "I figured this would be a place I could catch you without too many distractions."

I sucked my teeth and crossed my arms. "Can a girl get some privacy?"

"I've given you plenty of privacy," she said. "I haven't bothered you in a few hours!" Victoria pulled off her gray wig and unbuttoned a few buttons on her uniform. "Whew, it's hot under there! Anyway, darling, I saw in your meeting with Ms. West that you've gotten better at letting the truth just flow out of you."

"That's because every time I try to lie, you send stabbing pains to my head or food poisoning to my stomach, like I felt when I was looking at the debate team info sheet."

"I don't send those signals, my dear," Victoria said, putting a hand to her chest. "I send decidedly less painful ones. Your nose itching? That's me and my fairy dust. The other things you're feeling are your body's natural responses to stress—maybe you're feeling some anxiety. I'd imagine they're there to remind you to follow your heart."

She formed a ball of sparkles and dust and playfully bounced it in her hand, then put her broom down. "Now, it seems you still feel bad about not doing what your father wants you to do."

"How can I find the time to do what he *wants* me to do when I can't even do what's *expected* of me, like getting good grades?" I said. "I'm getting a C in math, and when he finds out, he will ground me for the rest of my life."

"Tell him what's really going on," Victoria said.

"I told him the truth about not wanting to do debate, and he basically threatened to disown me."

"Yes, but your body told you that you didn't want to do debate team. I saw it—you had your hands around your stomach like you were in pain! Isn't following your heart better than doing something you don't want to do?"

"Depends," I said. "I don't want to be an orphan."

Victoria stood next to me. "June, what do you think will happen if you tell your parents the truth?"

I turned toward her, and my eyes grew wide. "Disappointment. Anger. Sadness. Kicking me out and changing the locks—"

"June, dear, do you really think your dad would kick you out of the family? Do you think your parents would never speak to their own daughter again? They love you, and they want what's best for you."

She put her hand on my shoulder. "My dear, in the end, the truth—*your* truth—is what matters most. Lying to your father will be much worse in the long run than being real with him. You will lose his trust if you continue to lie. And trust takes a long time to regain."

The truth had already lost me my best friends. It had lost me my father's respect. Who knows what more damage I could do? "I don't know if I can be honest with him." I couldn't lose my dad, too.

Victoria reached out a hand and rested it on my shoulder. "Listen to your gut and speak from your heart," she said.

She stepped back toward the door. A plume of dust swirled around her like a mini tornado, circling her body until she disappeared. The dust faded away, and the gray wig and her uniform fell in a puddle in front of the cleaning cart. My fairy godmother was gone again, leaving me alone in the bathroom.

I stared at the cart, thinking about what to do. I still didn't want to tell the truth to my parents, even after Victoria's urging. But my head finally felt lighter after revealing my true feelings to her and Ms. West. After another five minutes in the restroom alone with my thoughts, I remembered why I'd gone there in the first place. I splashed some water on my face, and by then I really and truly had to pee.

✦

Later that night, I found myself locked in a battle with my own thoughts. Headaches, light-headedness, fast heartbeat. Every time I felt uneasy or confused about something, I experienced these weird physical symptoms. If it wasn't Victoria causing these things, where were they coming from? I went to the one place with the answers to everything: Google.

I typed things like "sweating," "rapid heartbeat," and "headache" into the search bar. A lot of scary things popped up in the results, including heart attacks (ain't I a bit young for those?!), aneurysms (arteries in your body expanding and maybe exploding!), and anxiety. (Wait, yes! Definitely! That's me. Anxious June. Should I change the name of my blog?) Then I stumbled upon panic attacks. The definition stuck out to me:

> *sudden episodes of intense fear that may cause physical reactions such as headaches, rapid or irregular heartbeat, shortness of breath, and trembling when there is no real danger or apparent cause*

The website went on to describe panic attacks as temporary and sudden, usually triggered by some stress or threat or something somewhat scary. "No real danger," it said. Perhaps the writer had never known the threat of a disappointed dad. Either way, now these panic attacks were just one more thing I was going to have to hide from everyone. I didn't want people to think I had issues! But that might cause even more panic. How much more would I be able to hold inside this overwhelmed, truth-telling body of mine?

HONEST June

CONFESSION #11:

That Victoria! She's literally everywhere! And this whole "living my truth" thing hasn't helped me live a better anything. In fact, it's added another level of stress. I'm already so worried over trying to get good grades, and not telling my dad about my bad ones, and keeping up with my after-school activities that I'm having panic attacks. And the mere idea of doing debate club gives me anxiety. I'm super freaked out about telling my dad I don't want to do it. I've *never* really told him no. Who am I to refuse my dad on anything? It's so much pressure to be a model kid. And now, under this dang spell, I have to tell the truth about everything. Even about my troubles in math class! I'll have to admit that I—*gasp!*—can't handle it all?!

No, I can't.

I just can't. If I admit that, it means everything

I've been trying to portray about myself—that I'm the perfect kid with perfect grades and big dreams, who makes their parents proud—is a lie.

Which means after all this . . . I haven't just been *telling* lies. *I've been living the lie.*

+ ✦

CHAPTER THIRTEEN

✦ ✦
✦

The Crab Shack was our family's local favorite spot. The outside patio had picnic tables, a white picket fence that wrapped around the entire restaurant, and a playground with a twisting slide that Nia and I used to hide on while our parents waited for the food to arrive. Indoors, the restaurant had soft booths and large tables, flat-screen televisions, and arcade games. The menu included seafood, barbecue, and flavored frosted drinks that came in cups that were as big as your head. I loved the biscuits; my mom loved the Cobb salad. My dad loved the fact the screens showed six football games at once in fall.

We settled into our usual booth near the bar, in plain view of the Georgia-Auburn game. A female server came over and offered us menus and drinks. "I'll have a lemonade," I blurted out. "Mom, should we just order the biscuits now?"

"Good idea," she said. "And I'll have an iced tea. Unsweetened."

I leaned back in my seat. I felt a certain tenseness in the air, especially between my dad and me. I could tell he was still mad at me about the debate team blow-up. I prayed he wouldn't bring it up again, so I wouldn't have to admit I hadn't signed up for the team yet—and wasn't planning to.

The server returned with the drinks and a warm basket of biscuits. I reached for one before she could even set the basket down on the table. I knew it was rude, but I was starving. "Thank you," I said to the server. She smiled. Her face appeared somehow different from the way it had looked before. More familiar. I couldn't quite explain how.

I took a bite of the biscuit, which was pure comfort food—ironic, since I was sitting across from my dad and feeling anything but comfortable. He reached for a biscuit, too. "These part of your field hockey training program?" he joked. I laughed nervously.

My stomach started to gurgle. Maybe it was the buttermilk in the biscuits. Or angst, thinking about what to say to my parents when they inevitably asked me about school. Just then, the server returned to our table with our appetizers. "Jalapeño poppers for the table," she announced. I turned to look at her face again. Yup, she definitely looked different. And was her hair different, too? She gave me a smile, a bit bigger than the last time. Why was my stomach so shaky?

"June," Mom began, "I haven't seen you much all week! How's school?"

Oh man, do we really need to get into this now?

"Everything's fine," I said. My stomach bubbled up in response, and my nose twitched. "Fine" was not how I felt just then. "Fine" in this context was basically code for "everything sucks." Of course, Victoria knew that. She was warning me.

"What do you mean, 'fine'? What's 'fine'?" Mom asked.

"Fine, as in fine, I wake up, go to class. Class is fine. Field hockey is much better now that Blake's on the team. And the school paper is great." That was all true. Somewhat. My stomach cramped again, and the smell of food started to make me feel sick.

"Field hockey practice is going okay?" Dad asked. "You sure? Your coach said you weren't as sharp the last few practices."

Well, Dad, little do you know, but I've had a bit on my mind these days. And when did you talk to my coach?! I thought. "Well, I've been going," I said.

"Being there and being fully present aren't the same things," Dad said cautiously.

"And what about your grades? Do I have to call a few of your teachers to get more details than just 'fine'?" Mom said.

"No, they're good," I told her. Another sharp pain in the gut.

"All of them?" she asked.

My stomach did a flip-flop. *Ugh, don't ask me about math, don't ask me about math*, I thought. Where's my phone? I'd type the real answer in my blog before I spoke.

But I didn't have time. Just as I found my phone, our server returned to the table and looked directly at me. *I knew it!* That smile, that glowing skin. It was Victoria. I let out an audible gasp at the table.

"Is something wrong?" Mom asked.

Victoria stood there, watching me, one of her eyebrows raised. I was the only one who could see her. My parents probably just saw the server who had come to our table originally—before Victoria morphed into her!

"You look like you've seen a ghost," Mom said. Which I basically had!

"No, nothing's wrong. I'm fine," I said in a rush. My stomach gurgled again, and nausea began to rise in my throat. I was going to be sick.

My mom shook her head. "You know, June, I don't think everything is quite right with you. You seem distracted

tonight. And at dinner the other night you seemed, well, preoccupied. Is something up?"

"Everything is fine," I said more forcefully, using that word again.

Victoria looked at me. Her forehead scrunched upward so four rows of lines were visible. My stomach started to burn as if the acid was eating through my stomach lining. I felt the word vomit rising. It became hard to breathe again. I clutched the collar of my shirt and looked over at Victoria in a panic, hoping she could save me from myself, but nothing could save me from the words that were about to suddenly cascade out of me.

In one flood of emotion, the word vomit released onto my parents. "I'm tired!" I shouted. "I'm tired of everything! I'm tired of the pressure. I'm tired of suggestions about how to live my life—what to study, what sports to play, what clubs to join, thinking about college and my career already! I'm eleven years old! No one has their life figured out by eleven! I'm tired of saying the right things, reading the right books, wearing the right things! I just want to be me, and live for me, and do me! Me. M.E.! June! Not Daddy's little girl, or Mommy's cute little princess, or Howard legacy, or third-generation anything! Me! I don't want to do the debate team, because I don't want to argue with people. I don't even want to be a lawyer! It feels like everything I've ever done has been to make *you* happy, not me!" I exploded.

Sweat beaded on my upper lip, and my clothes stuck to my skin. But now that I had partially unleashed, there was no way to stop me now. My dad's eyes shrunk to the size of M&M's (regular, not peanut), and his eyebrows turned in toward each other, touching in the middle of his forehead. My mother had turned quickly toward me at the beginning of my speech, her hair whipping around her head. Her mouth was open, but she was too surprised by my outburst to speak.

More word vomit rushed out of my mouth, with even more force than it had before. "Mom, I'm tired of you picking out my outfits! I'm not a baby, and I don't want to wear anything with bears or bows or Disney princesses or fat cartoons on it. I've been changing my clothes at school every day because I'm embarrassed to be seen in those outfits!"

"June!" my mom said in shock.

It was Dad's turn to feel my burn. "And I only play field hockey because Dad wants me to and because Blake's on the team. But if I could quit, I would quit that, too. All this 'it'll look good on your college résumé'—college is seven years from now! Why are you pushing me so hard? Why can't I just be a kid?! What if I don't even want to go to college? What if there *is* no such thing as college even by then? Plus, all these extra things are making it impossible for me to get good grades because they're taking up too much time!"

I took a deep breath and looked at Victoria, who gave me a reassuring nod. Her reaction triggered yet another confession. I looked my dad in the eye. "I got a C minus on my most recent math quiz, and I'm sure you're going to leave me here in this restaurant because no child of yours would ever get a C minus in life, ever!"

I sat back in my chair, spent. I felt like a deflated balloon—like all its pent-up air had just been released, and I'd flipped and flopped in the air haphazardly until coming to a rest in a pile on the floor. Although I probably looked lifeless, I felt weirdly refreshed. I had held on to my real feelings for so long—tensing my body and physically trapping my thoughts into an inner vault *for so long.* Releasing the truth about school—*about my C minus*— allowed my body to finally relax. Let go. Sit effortless for a change. My body felt like it was freer than it had been in a month. Gosh, maybe Victoria had been right all along. Maybe the truth could actually set me free. I felt guilty and humiliated about my outburst, but underneath those feelings was a new one, one I hadn't felt in a while: relief.

No one spoke for what seemed like minutes. I looked around and saw a few people at other tables looking in our direction, wondering what was going on. Dad tapped one finger on the table like there was an escape button he could push to erase the last two minutes of our conversation. He took a deep breath, his chest expanding broadly. His facial expression looked like he was about to discipline a disobedient dog.

"You got a C on a math quiz?" Dad asked.

"C minus. Yes, Dad. Less than average. And I know you don't do average," I admitted. Tears began to prick against my eyes, and I furiously wiped them away. I didn't want him to see me as weak—I'd be an even bigger disappointment to him than I already was.

Dad rocked back in his seat. "Okay. It's not ideal. But it's also early in the semester. You have plenty of time to study and get that grade up."

"Not if I do debate team," I said.

"Then why don't you drop the school paper?" he asked. "Besides, I don't think creative writing will take you on a path to the elite schools."

"What do you mean?" my mom asked. "They all love a creative. Plus, June's first story was on the front page of the paper."

"Yeah," my dad said. "But writing an article for the paper is not going to get her into Howard."

The word vomit rose in my throat once again. I looked at Victoria, my eyes wide, again hoping for a lifeline. I thought I'd unleashed everything I had to unleash! What more could I possibly reveal?! Instead, Victoria nodded and watched me dig myself into a bigger ditch as

I blurted out the most offensive words my father could ever hear.

"I don't *want* to go to Howard," I cried out.

Dad looked at me with the sharpest eyes I'd ever seen. That didn't stop the word vomit.

"Howard is *your* dream and *your* life. Not mine!"

I felt like I'd just bench-pressed my own body weight. I gasped for air, feeling a little faint. I'd just imploded eleven years' worth of hard work and good faith I'd built up with my parents. I'd never once been punished. I was a good kid! I followed the rules! My mom had raised her voice at me only a handful of times, when I had done something stupid. But what I just did, what I just said, certainly qualified as way more than just stupid. It was hurtful. It was almost *cruel*. A wave of guilt immediately crashed into me. Telling the truth? Yes, a good thing. But telling the truth by releasing the fury of a thousand men, screaming at my parents in the middle of a crowded restaurant, and making them feel like the worst humans on earth? Really unnecessary.

My dad sat silently in front of me. He didn't move even a nostril hair. He leaned back in the booth, pushing away his plate, and got up from the table. He went to the bar, ordered a drink, and tried to find peace in the football game. He never turned back toward our table.

My mother, trembling, looked at me. "I don't know

what has gotten into you, but the three of us are going to do whatever it takes to help you get your act together. And if that means taking away field hockey, school, friends, computers, phones, and TV, then so be it."

"Mom, I'm sorry. I'm just . . ." I searched for the right word to describe it. But my eyes must have said it all. She reached out and hugged me tight, holding me close against her chest to comfort me. "It's just too much."

"I know," Mom said.

She didn't know it all, but she knew enough.

Victoria watched as I sat with my mom, the tears finally flowing freely, letting out all the frustration that had built up in me for weeks. Maybe years. Maybe I'd been doing things to make everyone else happy for so long that I had lost myself. I wiped away my tears and sat upright for a moment, long enough to see that Victoria was wiping her thumb under her eye, too. I was the only one at the table that could hear them both say "It'll be all right," at the same time. I hoped that was true.

CONFESSION #12:

I knew this would happen.

I knew the truth would be too much for them. I knew my big mouth would get me into huge trouble. Now my parents, the most important people in my life, hate me. When I lied, it might have been more work to manage, but at least the people in my life were happy. In the moment anyway. Now I'm spilling my true feelings, and while it feels good to get it out, the people around me are not happy. Are they mad about my true feelings? Or mad that I'd been lying to them all this time? Or both?

Sigh.

It does seem slightly easier to breathe now. Maybe because I'm not holding so many feelings inside anymore? Like there's actually room for something inside my body other than secrets and stuff I don't want people to know? And I don't have any of those headaches or stomachaches or any of those other panic symptoms that I thought I would have if my parents found out about my bad grade and my not wanting to be a lawyer. Do I actually feel better now that I've told the truth?

And if I do, should I try to tell the truth more often, instead of trying to hide it?

And if I do, will the truth start to come out without this explosion of word vomit and without shocking my family and friends with an unexpected outburst?

And then will the truth be easier than lying?

And then will Victoria take away the curse?

I'm starting to understand what I need to do.

+ ✦

CHAPTER FOURTEEN

A fter my Crab Shack explosion, I wasn't
just grounded—I was on punishment. There was a
difference. To me, when you got grounded, you couldn't
have the things that help you leave the house—bike, car,
phone to text friends. But your life in the house could still
be fun. You might still be able to watch TV or play video
games. You might even keep your computer. And your
parents would still speak to you. But punishment meant
freedom in and out of the home was gone. All fun had
been taken away—no TV, no phones, no friends. And your
parents despised you. Or at least were so mad at you that
they couldn't look at you. Grounded was also short-term,
like a week or so. Punishment was multiple weeks, maybe
months. Maybe forever.

Dad channeled his inner Judge Joe Brown when he

told me what my punishment was. "You've insulted your mother and me, you've been lying to us, and you're not performing in school? You need some time? We'll give you time, little lady," he said once we got home. Two months in my room with no distractions is certainly time.

Mom and Dad argued over whether I should be allowed to do anything after school, like field hockey and the school paper. Dad wanted to pull me from the paper ("It's just another distraction," he said). But Mom persuaded him to let me continue pursuing it. "It's the school paper, not TikTok videos behind the football field!" she told him. "Let her stay on it. You never know—she could be the next Tamron Hall."

My mom was sad that my dad and I had hit a rough patch. Sad that I didn't communicate my true feelings earlier. Sad that this outburst maybe wouldn't have happened if she wasn't always at the hospital. "I feel like I've failed you, honey. I work too much. Maybe I've not spent enough time with you."

"You working didn't make me unhappy, Mom. Besides, I still see you every day."

"But then why, honey, haven't you been honest with us about your feelings before?"

I shrugged. "I was scared to tell you anything that might disappoint you. I didn't know if you'd be, like, ashamed of me. Or mad at me. But I had to be honest about everything now because I just felt like I was cracking. And I'm sorry it came out so badly."

"Well, I'm all for you telling us the truth, even when it's not what we want to hear. But it was the way you expressed yourself, honey." She paused, and the corner of her mouth lifted. "Exploding like that at the Crab Shack was not a good look. Who knows when your father and I can go back there again without the waitstaff pointing at us? Guess we'll have to get carryout from now on!"

Even I started to see my life in two parts: BC (Before Crab Shack) and AC (After Crab Shack). In BC, I was innocent, free, willing to sign up to the family's Howard legacy track. In AC, we don't look each other in the eye, and my parents consider me a waste of DNA who needed to be locked away out of sight, away from the public. Now I was stuck in my room, with nothing. Because I'd told the truth. I'd hurt my parents' feelings, but I'd told my truth. I'd told them their perfect valid hopes and dreams for me were trash. Ugh. I *did* deserve punishment.

In some way, I was really glad I had finally told them the truth. Punishment was awful—couldn't deny that part. But I also kind of deserved it. I'd been lying for a long time. And it had led to a huge, embarrassing outburst that my parents didn't deserve. I needed to be honest with my parents about being overwhelmed, because it was literally making me sick—the stomachaches, the headaches, the panic attacks. And since I'd told the truth I was feeling much better physically. Still, what had telling my truth solved, if now my dad wouldn't even talk to me? "The truth will set you free," Victoria had said. Why didn't it work like that in my case? Wasn't the effect supposed to be immediate? I'd told the truth, but I certainly wasn't free yet. And ever since I met Victoria and tried to live my truth, I'd only made a bigger mess of things. What if she was wrong? Or worse, what if she wasn't really looking out for me after all? What if her goal was really to wreak havoc on my life?

My thoughts spun. Then again, I realized—I didn't need Victoria to wreak havoc on my life. I did that part all by myself.

◆

I was dressed and ready to go to school Monday morning by 7:30. We didn't have to leave for school for another fifteen minutes, but neither of my parents came down early to chitchat or ask me what was on my schedule. I sat at the kitchen table, eating breakfast quietly, anxiously waiting for them to appear. Finally, at 7:44 a.m., my dad came downstairs. "I'll take you to school," he said awkwardly.

We rode to school in silence. The three-minute ride seemed like an eternity. Dad put on music in the car, preferring to listen to Snoop Dogg rap about the West Coast

doing their D-o-double-G thang rather than asking about my upcoming day. We pulled into the parking lot, and I turned to get out of the car as soon as possible.

"Class. Newspaper. Home. Mom will be waiting here at exactly four forty-five, after your meeting. Got it?"

"Got it," I said with a nod. It was only fair.

"Focus on your schoolwork," he said, and then turned to me and gave me a kiss on the forehead. "I love you. I'm still mad. But I love you."

My heart fluttered. After this weekend, hearing those words from him made me feel like I wouldn't have to pack all my belongings and find another home. It was like knowing your favorite flavor of ice cream was still in the freezer when you got home from school. Relief.

I walked toward the entrance of the school. I looked for Nia and Olive somewhere in the herd of students flocking to their first-period classes but didn't see them before I got to my locker. As I unloaded my books, Blake came up behind me.

"Hey, girl," she said in her perky tone. "How was your weekend?"

I looked at her. Her hair was pulled back into a smooth ponytail that hung down between her shoulder blades, and her eyes were wide and welcoming.

"You know, my life's just falling apart, no biggie," I replied. The honest truth, even to Blake. I couldn't hide my flaws anymore. I was on punishment. I was having panic attacks. I got Cs in math. I'd even lost my best friend's charm bracelet! I wasn't perfect, and I couldn't keep trying to pretend to be. And though I was still struggling with the idea that I wasn't as put together as everyone thought . . . it was better than holding it in and suffering, as I'd learned.

"What are you talking about?" Blake asked. "Is this about math?"

"It's more than just math," I said. "It's about math and science and field hockey and the school paper. And all of the things that I do on a daily basis to make my parents happy that I actually think make me miserable," I blurted out. I really wished I didn't have to recall this in the middle of school. But I knew Blake wouldn't let this go without some explanation. And Victoria's spell wouldn't let me hold it in. It was easier to just let it all out.

"What do you mean?" Blake asked as we walked faster toward math class.

"I basically confessed to my parents that I'm failing math, that I do not for the life of me want to join the debate team, that I don't want to go to Howard, and that I don't want to be a lawyer. I confessed all the lies I have told to keep them happy over the years. And they got pretty upset. And now I am on punishment. Which, honestly, I kind of deserved."

"Why did you have to confess all that?"

"Because I couldn't lie to them anymore."

"I'm sorry," Blake said, and it seemed like she genuinely meant it. "Is there anything I can do to help?"

"Help me run away from home?"

Blake giggled. "I've only lived here for a few weeks, June. I don't know my way around town that well."

Blake and I walked into math class and took our usual seats. Nia and Olive were sitting in the row closest to the door. Both of them looked at me, then looked away. I slithered into my seat two rows over from them, feeling more alone than ever. They didn't even know I was on punishment—Dad had taken away my phone, so I couldn't text or call them. Plus, they were still mad at me because they thought I'd abandoned our friendship.

But I hadn't. They were still my best friends. And though I'd been a dishonest friend to them, I hoped at some point they would forgive me, given my "condition" and all. I leaned over to get Nia's attention. "Psst! Pssssssst!"

Nia hesitated to turn around, but she finally did. "Girl, what?"

"You know I'm on punishment, right?"

Nia's eyes widened. She nudged Olive, who turned around, too. "No. What did you do?"

"I told my parents the truth about . . . everything."

"You told them about 'the thing'?" Nia asked.

"No! Not that. But everything else. And it didn't go well."

"I had no idea," she said, glancing at Olive.

"I haven't been calling you because I literally can't call you. They took away my phone. Best I can do is email you."

"I'm sorry," she said, and it sounded like she meant it. "How long is your punishment?"

"I have no idea," I said. "Until I graduate from high school?"

"I hope you can get out soon so we can, you know . . . talk and stuff."

"Me too."

They both gave me a little smile. Maybe they felt sorry for me. Maybe they had decided to forgive me. Either way, I'd take two people being even a bit less mad at me right now.

CONFESSION #13:

I finally told the unfiltered truth to my parents. I feel horrible about what I said—rather, how I said it. Here they've given me the best life I could possibly ask for, they love me to bits, and what do I do? Explode on them that I don't want to do any of the things they've made available to me.

But oddly, I do feel more relaxed now that I'm not carrying these pent-up feelings and frustrations inside my head. I wonder what would have happened had I let out little white truths this whole time? What if I had warmed my parents up to the fact that I maybe kinda sorta wanted to try things other than the debate team, or I also kinda liked other universities besides Howard, instead of exploding on them in a fit of rage with "DEBATE SUCKS!" and "BYE, HOWARD!"? Maybe I wouldn't have been so scared and anxious to let out the big feelings if I had let out little feelings first. Maybe the tension in my chest and those headaches I've been having lately wouldn't have been as bad. And maybe—oh man, I'd really hate to admit this—but maybe Victoria would have been right. Maybe she wouldn't have had to put me under a spell, because I would have already been telling the truth. Maybe she wouldn't have had to come into my life at all. Either way, it's starting to seem like I would have been better off telling the truth in the first place.

◆ ✦

CHAPTER FIFTEEN

In the early morning, I could hear my mother in her office listening to a podcast. I assumed it was by some tranquil doctor-like person talking about baby stuff. I paused at the door, standing behind the doorway so my mom couldn't see me. The voice coming through the speakers seemed quite familiar.

"So, you see, children's minds are going a mile a minute," the voice said. "The older they get, the more they're learning about concepts like logic, persuasion, and vulnerability. They learn how to vary their styles of communication, and they begin to understand the separation between their true inner feelings and what they communicate to others. Take the concept of truthfulness."

That voice. I recognized that voice. "When your child is lying to you, try not to think about the actual lie. Try

to think about the root cause of *why* they feel the need to lie."

Oh. My. Goodness. Somehow Victoria was talking through the radio directly to my mother about lies. About children lying. About *me* lying.

"Try to think, is there something going on with your child that would give them a reason to lie to you?" Victoria said in a calm, logical tone. "Is your child a pleaser, finding joy in making people happy? Or making you happy? Maybe the child thinks they only receive praise or attention from you when they are making you happy. Try to understand, and thereby sympathize with, your child, about why they lied, versus reprimanding them for telling the lie in the first place."

Victoria's voice continued to counsel my mom through my situation. I watched with my mouth wide open. I could not understand how I was the only one able to see Victoria, yet she was still able to communicate with other people when she wanted to. How unfair was it that she could be invisible *and* transform herself into other people? She should only have one superpower. This was Featherstone Creek, not a doggone Marvel comic!

My mother stopped and turned to her phone, then scribbled a note down on her legal pad. I stood near the doorway, watching her. Her face softened as she thought about what Victoria was saying. The only person I'd ever seen my mom listen to advice from this intently was Oprah.

I snuck downstairs and into the kitchen, opened the fresh box of bran flakes in the cupboard, poured out a bowlful, and splashed some almond milk on top. I took my bowl of cereal to the kitchen table. At this point, I'd eaten breakfast without scrolling through Instagram or texting my friends for more than a week already. Instead, I read school lessons or, sigh, the newspaper. Yes, we still got print copies. "People digest the facts better in print," Dad always said.

"Good morning," Mom said, arriving downstairs. She had her scrubs on already, meaning she was heading straight to the hospital, most likely to deliver a few babies. "Are you having anything to eat besides bran flakes?"

"Nope," I said. "Just flakes. I'll have a snack later."

"Okay," she said, "just want to make sure you eat enough."

Mom hesitated, then sat down in front of me. "So, June, I know it's been a rough week. I don't want to be mad at you forever. I do, however, want to understand why you felt you couldn't talk to us."

I looked away. This was going to be a heavy conversation for breakfast.

"I wanted to make you and Dad happy," I said. "So I did what you wanted me to do. Played field hockey, made good grades."

"Yeah, but you also have to be happy for yourself. What we want for you is to be happy."

I swallowed my last spoonful of bran flakes. "That's not how it always comes out," I said. "Dad is 'Mr. Howard.' You're a doctor whose dad's a doctor whose dad's a doctor. Your expectations for me are pretty obvious."

"That doesn't mean we won't be okay if you want to do other things. That we won't still love you."

"But when I got on the school paper, Dad treated it like a bother, and you showed little interest. Even when I made the front page."

"I was interested," Mom insisted. "I just didn't want it to interfere with your grades."

"And then when Dad wanted me to join the debate club, I told him the truth and he got mad," I countered.

"Well, he was disappointed, but that doesn't mean you should be forced to do debate if you truly don't want to."

"Well, tell him that," I insisted.

"I will," Mom said. She grabbed my hand. "Listen, I want you to be happy. Your happiness means the world to me. When you're happy, I'm happy. But you have to be happy for you. Not for us. If that means saying you don't want to do something, or you'd rather do something else, then just tell us the truth. It's on us to figure out how to live with it."

She continued. "Look, I know your dad has high expectations for you. And I do, too. I'd love for you to be a doctor, like me. But only if that will make you happy. There is more than one path to success, and I've seen that with my own family. We're full of doctors, lawyers, artists, writers, people who make furniture, people who buy and sell houses. Your cousin Earl cooks barbecue and runs a chain of successful restaurants! Makes more than your dad some years!"

"Really? From making ribs?" Earl Pierce ran Pierce's BBQ, which served the best ribs and coleslaw I'd ever had.

"Don't tell your father that. His ego, you know. But, yes, Earl sells his barbecue sauce at the supermarket and caters events and weddings. He served ribs at the Super Bowl last year. So, yes, he does well."

I relaxed my shoulders a bit. I could tell Mom's anger

had been defused by Victoria's guidance, and I was honestly grateful for her interference. "I'm sorry I lied before. I'm sorry about the Crab Shack. I just wanted to make you both happy."

"Oh, June," Mom said. "I'm happier now that you're talking to me."

✦

Blake was waiting for me at my locker when I got to school. "So, how are things at home?" Blake asked.

"Mom and I have pretty much made up. Dad is still mad at me. He can hold a grudge for, like, *ever*."

"He's a lawyer. He'll make his case against you until you crumble. How is math coming along?"

"Every day it's a struggle. Before, my excuse was not

having enough time. Now I have all the time in the world. But I just can't seem to focus."

"Maybe we can do a study session together? Even if it's virtual? Ask your parents if we can do something via Zoom if I can't come over."

"I'll try," I said.

My conversations with Nia and Olive weren't as comforting. I caught up with them after second period, and though the two of them seemed happy to see I wasn't completely depressed from loneliness, they were also kind of standoffish, as if they had more important things to do than talk to me.

Lunchtime was even more awkward. We'd gathered in the school cafeteria to take our normal seats together. It was the only social time I got with my friends, and I used all forty-five minutes of it to chat with as many people as I could. I tried having a conversation with Nia, but every time I asked her a question, I got a one-word answer.

"Did you see the new episode of *Black-ish*?" I asked.

"No."

"Did you see Alvin in science class? He looked good!"

"Nope," Nia said, then turned to Olive. "Did you see him?"

"Yeah. He got a haircut. Looked nice."

I took a bigger bite of my sandwich.

Nia cracked jokes about classes ("You see Kenya in social studies the other day trying to be extra with her answers?") and the fun but unproductive study session they'd tried to have at Nia's house that ended up with more videos for their TikTok feeds than actual homework completed. I wouldn't know what they posted on TikTok—I didn't exactly have easy access now that I was on punishment. I felt very left out.

Before classes started up again, I grabbed my school tablet and fired off a quick blog post, before I blurted out something I'd regret in front of Nia and Olive that would make things even more awkward:

CONFESSION #14:

How did this happen? I'm a complete outsider with my own friends. It's like they have their own secret language and only talk about things they've done without me.

I know I haven't been a great friend, but they could have been more understanding about me being so overwhelmed. I just want this fight to end already and for things to go back to normal! I hate feeling left out. I hate feeling like I don't know all the jokes. Or I don't know the words to a song! But I introduced Nia and Olive! They're friends through me! And now they act like I'm just an . . . acquaintance?

This is rough. I don't want to feel like I'm going through this alone.

After school and field hockey practice, I reported to my room. Both of my parents were at work; our housekeeper, Luisa, was home and made sure I got inside okay. My mom called from the hospital to check in.

"Am I allowed to have a virtual study session with Blake? We need to go over the next chapter for our math class."

She took a few moments to think about it. "Log on and only talk to Blake. I will check your computer afterward to make sure you stayed offline."

"Yes, ma'am." I sent Blake a note and an invitation to a Zoom link to set up our study date.

Within a few minutes, my computer screen filled with

Blake's smiling face. "Ready to dive into some formulas?" she asked, and I nodded. "Do you have your notes in front of you?"

"Yep," I answered.

"Cool. Let's start with the top of the lesson. You understand what's going on with the geometry formulas, correct?"

I looked at the words in the textbook. Then I looked at my notes. What I'd written did not resemble what was in the book. "I guess so?" I said. I figured I would get it once Blake explained it to me.

But as soon as the words came out of my mouth, I knew Victoria was listening.

I got that itchy feeling in my nose once again, like I had to sneeze. "I mean, well, not really. Can you explain once more?"

Blake broke down the formula into slow steps. "Then you calculate the area," she said. I followed her every move. "Got it." Yes, I did.

We continued on to the second formula. "Okay, now we need to solve for the area of a triangle. Do you know the formula for that?" I looked at my notes.

"Yeah," I said hesitantly, flipping through my notes. "All you have to do is take the height . . . and then, um . . . and . . ." I felt another urge to sneeze, like I'd just inhaled a bunch of dust. Dust! Fairy dust!

Blake looked up. "You don't really get it, do you?" she said flatly.

"No, I get it!" I blurted out. But I didn't really get it. I hated admitting I was wrong! The urge to sneeze was overwhelming, so I sneezed. And sneezed. And sneezed again! *Dang it, Victoria, with your messy, sneezy, wheezy, allergy-inducing fairy dust! Stop being right!* "Excuse me, sorry!" I said sheepishly.

Suddenly, the screen on my computer went wonky. It looked like somebody else was trying to call into our conference call. But I hadn't invited anyone else, nor had Blake. A notification popped up: "Would you like to accept Victoria into the call?"

I snatched my hands away from my computer. But the cursor dragged itself over to the Accept button and clicked. A third window appeared, and Victoria, pushing her face close to the camera and smiling and waving excitedly, was inside.

"What's wrong?" Blake asked.

"Nothing," I answered in a panic. That was a big fat lie. Victoria popping into view on the call was a huge something—something that literally could *not* be more awkward.

"June, my dear, why are you lying to your poor friend?" Victoria said, raising one eyebrow.

"SHHHHHHHHHH!!!!!" I hissed. "Can she hear you?"

"Of course not," Victoria replied, chuckling. Why was she laughing?! Nothing about her appearance on this conference call was funny! "Only you can hear me, my dear. But you need to tell her the truth about math."

"I'm trying!" I shouted.

"Try harder," Victoria said. "Confess your shortcomings. How are you going to learn the right way if you can't admit what you don't know?"

My face twisted in frustration. "I . . . argh! You're in the way! Can't you just leave?" I wanted to erase Victoria from this call. Couldn't I Ctrl+Alt+Delete her? *Argh!*

"You've made so much progress so far! You've been doing so well. I thought we had a breakthrough at the Crab Shack the other day. I was even considering lifting the spell then! Good thing I didn't. Remember, I'm just trying to keep you honest," Victoria said calmly. She sat back in her chair and waved her wand in front of her face. A trail of sparkly dust flowed from it. More dust started to fill the screen, and Victoria's window disappeared.

I gritted my teeth and reached my hands back up to the keyboard.

"June, is everything all right?" Blake asked. "You went mute, and it was like you were talking to yourself."

Victoria had left me to explain my bizarre behavior to Blake. My bottom lip started to quiver. I couldn't talk my way out of this. "I honestly am so lost that I don't even know where to begin."

That was true on so many levels.

Blake looked at me. "Take a breath. This math thing is not that serious. Let's go over every formula in this lesson and break it down bit by bit until you understand each one forward and backward. I have all night, and I will help you as long as I need to."

I covered my eyes with my hand. I was embarrassed that I needed such handholding to get me through a simple geometry lesson. I was even more embarrassed that I looked like I was talking to myself on the call. I never liked looking like I needed help or didn't have things under control. I was June Jackson! I used to handle everything! Even Lee said so.

But I wasn't handling anything right now.

I had no option but to study. I nodded at Blake and slowly ran my finger over the formulas I took notes on in class, nodding and listening as she re-explained our math lesson to me as slowly and simply as she could. We stayed on the conference call for close to two hours. I had to repeat a couple of the homework questions several times until I understood the formulas. I asked a lot of questions. I got frustrated, and then I realized where I was miscalculating. In between, Blake gave me helpful tips, and I eventually started to slow down. I took my time, fully comprehended each problem, and even figured out a few shortcuts. By the end of our session, I felt like I'd run a mile, but I was ready to handle our next quiz. Blake's help had gotten me there, and none of it would've been possible had I not told her the truth about my trouble with math at school.

In that moment I realized something—something big and important. I logged into my blog and began to type.

HONEST June

CONFESSION #15:

I don't think I have the energy to hide the truth from people anymore. And you know what? It might be a good thing. I'm finally ready. I let my parents know my true feelings about school and college and everything else, and my mom has been supportive. Recently we've talked more than we have in a long while! And because I admitted I was clueless about our math lesson, Blake helped me study. Now I feel way better about my homework. Maybe part of telling the truth is admitting when I don't have it 100% together all the time—that I need help sometimes. And maybe admitting I need help isn't a sign of weakness, either. Maybe help is exactly what I need to keep it all together most of the time.

Victoria was right—and that's the truth.

CHAPTER SIXTEEN

✦ ✦
✦

I don't know if it was Victoria, a prayer to God, or some other blessing from the universe. But proof that miracles do happen fell onto my desk in math class when Mrs. Charles handed back our quizzes. An A minus. Praise be.

I looked over at Nia and Olive and mouthed the words "A minus." Olive gave me a thumbs-up and a wide smile, and Nia tilted her head to one side as if to say, "It's about time!" With this grade, I might be able to speak to my father again without being terrified of what his reaction would be.

The school bell rang, and Blake walked over to my desk. I threw my arms around her shoulders. "Thank you so much! Because of you I might not have to move out of my house."

"Very funny," Blake said. "But I didn't do anything. It was your hard work. This should prove you can do anything you want if you just focus."

"That sounds like something my parents would say."

We walked out of class together, shoulder to shoulder. Nia and Olive huddled by the door, and as we crossed the threshold, Nia turned to me and raised one eyebrow. "June, are we going to second period together?"

A silence hung between the four of us, the realization sinking in that Nia's invitation did not include Blake. Blake didn't stay around long enough to wait for one. "I'll see you later, June. Good luck with the rest of your day."

"See you later, Blake," Nia said in a phony-cheerful tone.

I turned to look at Nia. "Girl, what was that about?"

"What? She's not in our next class!"

"You didn't have to be so rude!"

Nia rolled her eyes. "Girl, whatever. We going or what?"

I felt the muscles in my throat become tense and my fingers clasped together. I couldn't believe she'd spoken to Blake like that. I backed away from Nia, feeling more annoyed with every step. "I need to go to my locker first. I'll meet you there."

I needed to get the book for science class—that was true—but I also needed to release the word vomit before I blurted out something to Nia that would make her hair frizz. I walked quickly to my locker, opened the door, and pulled out my cell phone to fire off an entry in my blog.

CONFESSION #16:

Mirror, mirror on the wall, who's the meanest of them all? Nia Shorter, y'all.

We've had so many good times together, and I'd hoped for so much more, but she's been so hurtful lately, and I'm starting to question if I even want to be friends with her at all. Nia has really crossed the line. Her attitude toward Blake is so nasty, and I can tell Nia's super jealous of her. What's not to be jealous of? Blake's tall, pretty, and well traveled. And she gets perfect grades and speaks like an adult. And best of all, she's understanding and kind. She helped me when I most needed it. But when

I most needed Nia's understanding and kindness, she ignored me! Nia is my best friend, but I wish she wouldn't act like such a mean girl. Why is she such a hater? Maybe she needs to loosen up those braids— they might be cutting off circulation to her brain.

✦ ✦

I tossed my phone back into my book bag. Just then, Nia came up behind me. "Coming?"

I jumped nervously. "Yeah, I told you I had to get something from my locker."

"I heard."

I walked in front of Nia toward science class and didn't look back at her until we took our seats.

✦

I was excited to come home after school for the first time in days. Our family dinners had been very quiet. Mom and Dad would talk about their days briefly, but when I tried to jump in, he'd turned silent.

Tonight, I brought my math quiz with me to dinner. I put it on his plate before he could sit down. When he came over to the table, he paused and picked up the quiz.

His eyes widened. The eyebrows moved a half centimeter toward his hairline. I could actually see a toothpick's width of skin in between them.

"Ah, that's more like it," he said. "Nice work." He placed it on the side of his plate and nodded. Then he dug into the chicken pot pie Mom had made for dinner.

I sat up straighter as I ate my pot pie, blowing on each creamy bite of chicken and vegetables before I popped it into my mouth. I hadn't had much of an appetite lately, despite my mom cooking my favorite meals—mac and cheese, pizza poppers, sweet potato fries. It was hard to eat with my dad frowning at me like he was still angry with me.

"June, great job, honey. See, she's getting it together," my mom said to my dad, trying to get him to cut me some slack. His face looked softer, like he was enjoying both the food and all the company present at the table. He looked over at me more than once as I ate. "Good, right?" he asked, almost shyly.

I looked at him in the eye, for the first time in many days without fear. "Yeah, this is good."

HONEST June

CONFESSION #17:

The wall has come down. The ice has thawed. I see a light at the end of the tunnel! I think maybe, just maybe, Dad might not be mad at me anymore. All because I got an A– on my math quiz.

Ah, wait. . . . Actually, I got the better grade because I admitted to Blake that I needed help with my math work. So . . . I guess the truth got me here. Maybe I don't have to have it all together, all the time. Maybe leaning on others sometimes is good for you. I mean, hey, I can't win a field hockey game by myself. It's a team sport. Maybe I need my own team to help me live my best life? Like my friends. And my parents. And . . . I can't believe I'm going to say this . . . Victoria.

CHAPTER SEVENTEEN

✦✦
✦

The temperature in our house must have warmed up by twenty degrees that night. As dinner went on, Dad asked me questions, real questions, about my life. He asked if I could download YouTube videos on my school tablet (yes), if Lee still had his pet lizard (also yes), and if the girl at the end of the block was having a car wash fundraiser for cheerleading, because he wanted to get the Mercedes polished "for a good cause" (last I heard, it was on Saturday morning). He didn't ask me anything about grades or even mention the word *Howard*. Things almost felt normal in the house again. I even ate most of my chicken pot pie, my appetite finally back.

After dinner I went upstairs to my room to get a jump on my studies. I flipped through my English literature reading and my science homework, doing my hardest to focus, but I found my thoughts straying to Nia and Olive and Lee. A knock on the door snapped me back to reality. Dad was standing in the doorframe. "Congratulations on your math quiz," he said. "It's good to see you getting good grades again."

"Thank you," I said, surprised to see him there, looking like he actually wanted to chat.

Dad walked into the room. I couldn't remember the last time he was in here for longer than a few seconds, looking at the knickknacks I'd collected on my shelves and dressers. He looked around at the pictures I'd posted around—of Nia and me at Disney World, of Lee and me at the lake, of him and Mom and me in Paris. I'd taped a new concert poster from Beyoncé's latest tour above my desk.

"When I was your age, I had concert posters of Sade and Prince in my bedroom," he said. "Funny how time flies."

I didn't understand if this warm banter meant I was off punishment, so I stayed silent, wary of what was coming next. He sat down on the bed and gestured for me to come sit next to him.

"Listen, June," he began, "I know I'm tough on you. I have high standards for you. But it's only because I love you. And because I want the best for you."

I looked at his face. The eyebrows had drawn away

from each other and settled evenly over each eye like hairy caterpillars. The skin in between the eyebrows was smooth. He put his hands on his knees.

"You know why I love Howard so much?" he began. "Because it was one of the few places where I wasn't the only Black person in a room. I was one of the only Black kids in my high school. And at my law firm back in New York. When I met with clients, people would often overlook me, thinking that I was just a paralegal or an office assistant. They would never guess that I was a practicing attorney, let alone the lead attorney on their account!"

I bit my lip. I couldn't imagine anyone mistaking my dad for anything but a lawyer. Suits? Check. Briefcase? Always. The swagger of Billy Dee Williams slash Uncle Phil from *The Fresh Prince of Bel-Air*? Checkity-check. Those fools must have been blind.

"When I was a kid and I was applying to college, one of the guidance counselors at my school told me that I had to be twice as good just to get half as far, especially as a Black man in this country. And that stuck with me. So I worked my hardest. I got straight As in high school. I participated in all the extracurriculars I could, just to give myself an edge. I got into Howard, got straight As again. I worked my way into law school and got a law degree, JD, summa cum laude. And when I had achieved all those things and became an associate at one of the most successful law firms in New York, I went back to that counselor and I told him, 'Look, I worked twice as hard. I made it.' And he laughed at me. He said, 'Yeah, you worked twice as hard, and yet you still probably make half as much.' When you work for someone else—at a law firm, or a clothing store, or a newspaper, or anywhere—you will always be undervalued."

I nodded slowly. I had no idea it was so hard for him to get where he was. I was glad he was telling me his truth.

Dad continued. "I left the firm, moved to Featherstone Creek, and started my own firm with my best friend. And we make a great living. We make what we're worth. And together, we have not only made more money but also created a foundation and a legacy for our families' future successes."

I blinked. So, my dad's office was a gift for Nia and my futures? That put anything Santa had brought me for the last, like, eight Christmases to shame. Dad's work was for me? Wow.

I realized that everything Dad had done—even when he was being tough—was to help set up a future for me. I suddenly felt a rush of gratitude and appreciation. He was trying to take care of me the best way he knew how. But I wondered if I had to accept these gifts. At least in their current form.

"Dad, you're an awesome lawyer. You're built to be a lawyer. What if I'm not?"

He rocked back on the bed, then leaned forward again.

"Then, June, that's okay. But I don't want you to settle for being less than exceptional. I think you can be a great lawyer. But if it's not your thing, I'll let it go. I want you to work hard at achieving whatever you want to achieve, because I want you to be so good at whatever you do that people can't say no to you. They can't deny you anything. That's what I'm trying to ingrain in you."

"I get it, Dad," I said. I did, I really did, and I really cared. "But I'm also only eleven, and I have feelings and thoughts, too."

"I know. I get that now. That's where I've gone wrong. You *are* just eleven, and you *do* deserve the time to make mistakes and figure things out on your own." He raised an eyebrow. "But you can't just explode on me at the Crab Shack. You were still out of line."

"I know and I'm sorry," I said. I felt way more connected with Dad after he'd confessed the struggles he had growing up. It was like he was trying to prepare me for the challenges of the world so I could be in an even better place to face them than he'd been in when he was my age.

I smiled at him. "So where do we go from here?"

"Well, how do you really feel about things?"

I took a deep breath. Telling the truth had not paid off well for me in the past few weeks. But I think I was ready to try again. Now that we were having an honest conversation, for the first time maybe ever, I wanted to tell my dad the truth. He'd been straight with me, so it was only fair that I be straight back at him.

"Which things?" I asked, ready to talk.

"Let's start with debate. You're really not feeling that one, right?"

"No, Dad," I admitted.

"Right. What about field hockey?"

My shoulders tightened. "Let's see how the season goes," I said.

"I hope you won't let that talent go to waste. Coach says you're a natural."

"And what about us?" I asked. Extracurriculars and school was one thing, and it had definitely been overwhelming me lately—but nothing made me feel worse than thinking my dad didn't want anything to do with me anymore. We had to fix this.

"How about we find time for a little dinner outing here and there to talk, just the two of us?"

"I'd love that. Where?"

"Well, it sure ain't gonna be the Crab Shack, that's for sure!" he said.

My face fell. "You really think we'll never be able to go back there, for real?" I begged. "I can't live my whole life without those cheddar garlic biscuits!"

"Maybe you and I can spend some time finding another regular family spot?"

He gave me a kiss on the cheek and smiled. It felt like the concrete wall he'd put up between us had finally been knocked down, and I could see him standing on the other side. "Does this mean I'm not on punishment anymore?" I ventured hopefully.

"Nope. You still are. Back to those books," he said, walking toward the door. Then he turned around to wink at me. Both eyebrows moving independently! A sign from the universe that things were going back to normal! He closed the door again, leaving me alone with my thoughts.

I reached for my laptop. I felt like I had won. I typed an entry in my secret blog.

CONFESSION #18:

Dad's no longer mad at me. I thought he'd never come around. I really thought he'd make me move out. Where would I have gone? Fled to Nia's house? Moved in with Lee? See, I knew the universe was pushing us to be together.

Anyway, all good now at home. Actually, really good. My dad and I had one of those family sitcom conversations where the kid admits they did something wrong, the parent admits they're disappointed, but everyone hugs it out in the end. Sharing my true feelings got Dad and me to a better place. He even shared the truth with me! And I had no idea about all that stuff he had to go through when he was growing up. Funny—he told his truth and now I understand him more. I told my truth, and he gets me more. The truth got us both to a better place.

Okay, Victoria, you win. It won't always be easy, but honesty is going to be my new policy from here on out. Now will you lift the spell?

✦

CHAPTER EIGHTEEN

L ee stopped me in the hallway on Friday
as we were walking to fourth period. "Hey, is Sunday
dinner open? It's been a minute since we broke bread."

Lee hadn't been over to our house since before I was
put under the spell, and I really missed hanging out with
him. Luckily, it seemed Lee had missed coming to our
house, too. I was relieved he'd asked about Sunday dinner. I didn't want to invite him myself, because then it
might look like I was asking him on a date. Or something.
I didn't know how dates work, but I imagined me saying
"Would you like to come to my house for dinner?" would
result in the kind of blushing and nervousness that I'd feel
on a date.

"Yeah, it's free," I said, trying to stay cool and say as

little as possible before the truth came vomiting out of my mouth. "Come through, same time, same place."

✦

On Sunday afternoon, that blouse from Fit finally saw the light of day. I put it on with jeans for dinner and threw on a gray sweater, knowing Mom would inevitably ask me to put one on when it got cooler as the sun set. "You look nice," my mom said as I came down to help with dinner.

"Thanks," I responded. She smiled and turned back to chopping carrots. I felt my chest puff up with confidence.

The truth about me not loving the clothes my mom had picked out had earned me some newfound fashion freedom. It's as if Mom appreciated my point of view and let me wear what I wanted. And she wasn't in any way bothered by it. I was happy. Mom was cool. Point for Victoria.

I was nervous about hanging out with Lee, and I couldn't help but worry I would say something to scare him away, especially since my feelings were a wide-open book these days. It was bad enough he thought I was a dunce at math. He was starting to see I didn't have it all together, which was already super embarrassing. But what if I blurted out that I thought about us as more than friends? Like, as bf/gf? Or as parents—I'd daydreamed often about what our kids could look like, and I was sure they'd have my eyes and his smile. I wasn't sure I wanted to kiss Lee right now, but I couldn't stop myself from thinking about our future possible kisses together.

Lee's grandparents dropped him off for dinner at 5:00 p.m. on their way to bingo, and Mom said we'd bring him back home when we were done. Dad grilled up beef and turkey burgers, and Mom had made mac and cheese and a spicy coleslaw. The 7UP cake was already on the cake stand on the counter, where Mom stood pouring the icing just as Lee walked through the door. He kissed his two peace fingers and pointed at the cake when he walked in. "Blessings, fam. You and I will reunite later."

Sitting down at the table next to Lee felt comfortable.

My dad smiled at me as he served me a burger. Then he turned to Lee. "Lee, you bulking up? Shall I do one or two burgers for you?"

I wondered how many more times my dad would make these corny jokes. We had at least seven more years of dinners like these before we went off to college. Lee laughed and nodded, and Dad put a turkey burger and a beef burger on his plate.

"Lee, what's going on at school?" Dad asked casually.

"It's all good, you know. June and I have a few classes together. I'm in the Creeks club too, doing work down at the river to save the animals and clean things up."

"That's wonderful." My mom beamed. "These kids and their extracurriculars. You all amaze me at every turn."

He amazed me, too. I stared at Lee. I studied his face. His cheeks. His smile. I smiled. I felt this weird sensation in my chest that could have been indigestion, or anxiety, even. But it didn't hurt. It felt like I had drunk a mug of hot chocolate. Warm, sweet. I'd never felt this before. Was this some weird signal from Victoria pushing me to tell Lee what I was feeling? Dang it! *Shake it out, shake it out, June!*

"I'm going to the restroom!" I said, maybe too loud and too eager. I took care to keep my phone in my pocket during dinner, just in case I felt the urge to word vomit about anything during the meal, particularly about Lee. (Although I'm technically still on punishment, my dad allowed me to keep my phone to use for "emergencies."

Preventing word vomit counted as an emergency, right?) I jumped up from the table and dashed into the bathroom across from the kitchen. Once safely locked inside the bathroom, I quickly typed into my phone.

HONEST June

CONFESSION #19:

Lee. I don't know what's happening. All I know is when he's around, I feel better. I feel better than better. I feel like I've eaten cotton candy, and sugar and glitter are tickling my chest. My dad is happier and makes jokes. My mom smiles more and looks more relaxed. Everything is lighter. And Lee's laugh makes me laugh. What is this? Is this a crush? Is this LOVE? Like my mom and dad's love? I've never even kissed anyone! How will I know if I'm doing it right? Does this mean we will get married and have kids? Okay, relax, June. Breathe. First things first—how will I ever know if he feels the same way?

I splashed some cold water on my face and forced myself to think about other things. Math. Field hockey formations. We needed more hand soap in this bathroom,
too. That's what I'd do. I'd walk back to the dinner table
and tell Mom we needed more soap. That was my mis-
sion. *Stay focused.*

I opened the door and went back toward the patio.

"Who wants cake?" my mom asked. "Lee, I know
you're in. June?"

Another test of truth. I couldn't fake liking that dry
pound cake anymore. I promised my mom I'd be honest
about my feelings. "I'll pass. I'm not feeling cake today."
That was true.

Mom turned toward the kitchen without so much as bending a finger crookedly at me. That wasn't bad! I could be honest about my feelings and not have the world burn down.

Lee and I lingered next to the table while my dad helped clear the plates. "So, your girl Nia. How is she doing?" he said casually, picking at his cake with his fork.

I looked at him. My heart fell a few inches in my chest. In all our years being friends I'd never heard him ask about "my girl Nia." Why all of a sudden did he care how she was doing? And should I tell him the truth? That she's gulping down haterade by the gallon and spitting it on Blake and me?

"Dunno, haven't seen her since school," I said, my eyes shifting to the side.

"You didn't kick it all weekend?"

"Nope, had field hockey and homework last week, and technically I'm still on punishment." I paused. "Why are you asking about Nia?"

"Oh," Lee said awkwardly. "Nothing."

"Right, 'nothing.' Spill it. Does Alvin like her?" I interrogated.

"Alvin?" Lee jerked his head back. "Um, I . . . don't think so? He's never mentioned her. Or any girl, like ever. Only talks about video games. Never mind."

Lee finished his slice of cake. I carried his plate toward the kitchen, gritting my teeth, desperate to hold in my true feelings about his questions about Nia. I shoved his plate into the sink and scrubbed it hard with soap and water, trying to wash away both the crumbs and my wishy-washy, lovey-dovey feelings for him.

But afterward, while we hung out on the patio chatting about his pet lizard, and as I watched his grandparents pick him up from our house, that fluttering in my chest was still there.

✦

Nia texted me just as I went upstairs to get ready for bed. (A late-night text from a best friend counts as an emergency, right?)

NIA: Hey girl.

JUNE: Hey.

NIA: Been a minute. You good?

JUNE: Yeah. Sunday dinner wasn't the same without you. Lee was here.

NIA: Lee, huh? I'm sure you liked that.

I didn't know what she was getting at. What did that mean?

NIA: You know what I mean. Dinner with your boy Lee. Did you hold hands? Kiss on the trampoline?

JUNE: Girl, no! He's my friend.

My heartbeat jumped.

NIA: That's all right. I know where you hide your true feelings.

What the—? Nia knew about the spell, so she knew I couldn't lie. But did she know about the blog? Did she see me typing in it at school the other day? My mind raced. Crap. If she knew about the blog, then she'd know how I felt about Lee. And the—eeeek!—awful things I'd said about her, too.

I changed the subject quickly, hoping to distract her.

> **JUNE:** You talk to Alvin?

> **NIA:** Why would I talk to him?

> **JUNE:** Well, aren't you, like, into him?

> **NIA:** Not really. Oh! What's up with my bracelet? I know you've had a lot going on, but I wanted to make sure you didn't sell it on eBay or something.

Oh man. I forgot I still hadn't told her the truth about losing it. Great. I had to tell her, but it was just going to give her another reason to be mad at me.

> **JUNE:** Yeah, about that. I didn't sell it.

I took a breath.

> **JUNE:** I lost it. I'm so sorry. I wanted to replace it by now, but with everything going on, I haven't had time.

> **NIA:** Juuuunnnneeeee. . . . . . .

There was a long pause. Great. She was probably deleting my number from her phone now. What more could I do to betray this friendship?

She texted back:

> **NIA:** Girl, it's okay. There was a rhinestone missing from one of the charms anyway. I'll send you links for another one I found that I liked. My birthday's coming soon. 😊

My hands relaxed around my phone. That was the complete opposite of the reaction I was expecting from her. I sent her a smile emoji in return and vowed to save up some of my allowance money to grow the Nia Shorter Bracelet Replacement Fund as fast as possible.

✦

I felt like I was heading back on track with Nia after our text exchange. I FaceTimed Chloe with some—um, emergency—updates.

"I'm freeeeee!" I said excitedly.

"Oh, thank goodness," Chloe replied. "So now what? Nia speaking to you yet?"

"Somehow, yes. Lee was just here. That was . . . interesting."

"Interesting?" Chloe said, her voice raising an octave. "Since when is Lee interesting?"

"Since . . . he's one of my closest friends. He's always been cool."

"Cool, yes, but not interesting. Do you *like* him? You should tell him! You still under that spell?"

I started sweating. I had that glittery feeling inside again. This was one truth I didn't know if I was strong enough to reveal. Yes, the truth had helped me forge a better relationship with my parents (and I was working on things with Nia and Olive), but telling Lee how I felt about him seemed too big for me to handle.

"Ugh, yes, I am. It actually proved to be a good thing. I told my parents how I really felt, and though it was awkward, in the end we're back on track. And I can pick out my own clothes and do the after-school stuff I want. But I haven't tested the theory out when it comes to romance. Isn't romance and dating and stuff all about hiding your feelings? Making the other person chase them out of you?"

"You need to stop watching those dating reality shows. Does your mom know you watch those? Anyway, wouldn't it be easier to be honest?"

In matters of grades, Howard, dress codes, and food preferences, yes. I'd certainly learned that lesson. But Lee? My chest tightened. My breathing became faster than normal. "Maybe," I responded.

I hung up with Chloe and tossed my phone onto the bed and threw myself down into my comforter. I looked at the ceiling and took a few deep breaths. I closed my eyes for a second, hoping that would help me clear my thoughts.

But she had heard me. A plume of dust seeped up from under the door, and glitter scattered all over my bedroom floor. The tornado formed right in front of me, a flurrying funnel of stardust. Beyond the stupid spell, the second most annoying thing about Victoria was that she made such a mess when she came into a room.

"Hello, my dear!" she said, wiping down her dress and standing on one foot. One of her sparkly shoes had slipped off her foot when she arrived, and Victoria hobbled over to the other side of the room to grab it and put it back onto her foot. "Oh, gosh, that dust! Does a number on my allergies, too."

Victoria smoothed her hair back from her face and rubbed her nose. "So, I see you've made nice with your father. See, my dear, I told you that everything is better when you tell the truth." She sat down at the end of the bed. "But I also heard what you told Chloe about Lee. Be careful, my June. Don't slip back into your old ways."

"I won't," June said. "Haven't I shown you that I can tell the truth easily now? I did what you asked me to. I've learned my lesson! So now will you lift the spell?"

Victoria walked around my room, looking at my grade-school trophies and ribbons for spelling competitions and writing and reading achievements. She walked in front of me and leaned back on my desk. "Our relationship is not quite done," she said decisively. "You've got one more thing to do before I can drop the spell."

"No more deals," I begged. "That's how I got into this mess in the first place!"

Victoria leaned in. "In order to get out of this 'mess,' as you call it, you've got to prove to me you can go without a single lie, half-truth, or purposeful omission. Then I'll drop the spell." She crossed her arms resolutely, accidentally poking herself in the cheek with her wand in the process.

"But I'm already doing that," I cried.

Victoria straightened up. "Practice makes perfect, June. You haven't really reached a point where the truth is flowing through you naturally. I think at times you still see it as a point of weakness. But it's not—remember what I told you when we met? It's a superpower."

Honest June. Super June. I like the sound of that, actually. But the truth, the unfiltered truth, at all times? Who knew what awful things I'd say next? Maybe this time I'd tell Mrs. Charles that her breath smells of stale coffee and bacon bits. Or I'd roll up on the athletic director and tell him to shove his budget for girls' and boys' sports in the shredder and start over! Maybe I'd get myself suspended and shipped off to a boarding school, where I'd be beaten up by the older kids and have no contact with anyone from Featherstone Creek ever again!

"June, you've come this far," Victoria said. "You've already confessed some of your biggest secrets. Things certainly can't get much worse. But now that you know the power of your words, use them to empower yourself, not to make yourself feel weak. Remember, the truth is a superpower."

Victoria twirled around in the middle of my room, spinning faster and faster until she turned into a blur. A pile of pixie dust collected where she once stood. But this time, the pixie dust crawled into a trail toward my bathroom, then gathered in a pile in front of the mirror. A trail. A map.

I followed the dust into the bathroom, careful not to step on it. I was unsure whether these were actual ashes of Victoria or just fairy dust bread crumbs leading me. I sidestepped the dust puddle in the bathroom. Would she reappear and spin from these same ashes at some point? Or could I just leave this for Luisa to clean up in the morning? If Luisa could even see Victoria's dust.

I stood in front of the mirror. My jaw clenched. I couldn't see Victoria, but I closed my eyes before she could appear in the glass unexpectedly.

"The truth is simple. The truth is easy. The truth . . . is me," I said just above a whisper, loud enough to be heard by Victoria if she was listening.

I waited a few moments. I felt my heart flutter, then settle in my chest. I expected the hairs on my arms to stand up or a shiver to move up my spine. Or at least the lights to flicker. Instead, everything was still. I felt a weird sense of calm. Like I was firmly rooted with my feet on the ground.

I opened my eyes. I said it again, slightly louder this time. "The truth is simple. The truth is easy. The truth . . . is me."

I looked at the pupils of my eyes. I felt like I could see through my head and into my brain. Everything there seemed calm, too. And still. *Am I dead? Nope, I'm breathing. Slowly, but breathing.* I felt normal. Okay. Like, ready for whatever would happen next. I didn't look around for Victoria. I wasn't worried about my parents or grades or school. I wasn't thinking about field hockey or Nia or Lee or my future. I had not one worry or thought on my mind in this exact moment. I didn't know if this spell had erased my thoughts or reprogrammed my brain in some way. But for this instant, I felt like something had been lifted off my shoulders—if not the spell, then *something*.

I looked away from the mirror and took a step back. I only heard the hum of the lights above the sink. Just me.

I turned toward the door. The dust below me was gone.

I heard a faint recognizable voice whisper back from the mirror, "The truth will set you free."

Acknowledgments

I will forever be grateful to Kate Udvari and Ann Maranzano for their support and partnership. To Sasha Henriques and Michelle Nagler, thank you for helping me bring June Jackson to life! It has been such a pleasure to work with you, and I can't wait to see where June's adventures take her.

Stef, I am so lucky to collaborate with you. Thank you for all the late-night sessions and marathon calls. I couldn't ask for a better writing partner.

Brittney, thank you for your beautiful illustrations. I know my readers will fall in love with them, too.

To André Des Rochers, Bejidé Davis, and the entire Granderson Des Rochers family, thank you for your continued support and counsel throughout this process.

To Phoebe, thank you for all the texting and FaceTiming

to help me get June just right. It's my honor and privilege to write for you and girls just like you.

To my family: Mom, Dad, Adrianne, Erica, Lisa, and William, I am lucky to be a member of the best tribe. Thank you for all your love and support.

To Cristiano, eu te amo sempre. As we always say, "sempre juntos."

To Michelle, I thank you always because I just wouldn't survive without you! You are the best cousin/friend a girl could ask for, and I had Blake in mind the entire time I was working on this project.

To all my dear friends, I am so lucky to do life with you. Thank you for the laughter and love that fuel my creativity.

Finally, to my readers, there will never be enough thank-yous for your emails, posts, and support. Here's to more writing adventures.

ABOUT THE AUTHOR AND ILLUSTRATOR

Tina Wells is the founder of RLVNT Media, a multi-media content venture serving entrepreneurs, tweens, and culturists with authentic representation. Tina has been named one of *Fast Company*'s 100 Most Creative People in Business, has been listed in *Essence*'s 40 Under 40, and has received *Cosmopolitan*'s Fun Fearless Phenom Award, among many honors. She is the author of nine books, including the bestselling tween fiction series Mackenzie Blue; its spin-off series, The Zee Files; and the marketing handbook *Chasing Youth Culture and Getting It Right*.

◆

Brittney Bond was born in sunny South Florida to a Jamaican family. A self-taught artist, she works primarily digitally, with a passion for using appealing color palettes, intriguing lighting, and a magical and positive aura throughout her illustrations.

June is lucky enough to score the leading role in the school musical, but the offstage and onstage drama threatens to topple everything. Will she be able to overcome Victoria's curse in time for opening night?

The truth will set you free in the next book in the Honest June series!

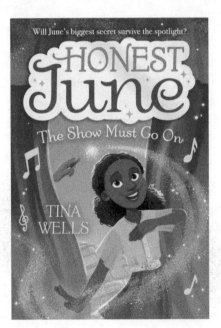

Available Summer 2022!